A NEW TESTAMENT

T0243725

A New Testament

Novel

Devakanthan

translated from Tamil by
Nedra Rodrigo

MAWEN𝒵I
HOUSE

Copyright © Kalachuvadu Publications
English translation Copyright ©2024Arundathy Rodrigo

Except for purposes of review, no part of this book may be reproduced in any form without prior permission of the publisher.

We acknowledge the support of the Canada Council for the Arts and the Ontario Arts Council. We also acknowledge the support of the Government of Canada through the Canada Book Fund.

We acknowledge the financial support of the Government of Canada through the National Translation Program for Book Publishing, an initiative of the *Roadmap for Canada's Official Languages 2013-2018: Education, Immigration, Communities*, for our translation activities.

Cover design by Sabrina Pignataro
Cover photo by Pirunthajini Pirabakaran
Author photo by Aiya 4U

Library and Archives Canada Cataloguing in Publication

Title: A new testament : novel / Devakanthan ; translated from Tamil by Nedra Rodrigo.
Other titles: Kanavuc cirai. Oru putiya kālam. English
Names: Tēvakāntan, 1947- author. | Rodrigo, Nedra, translator.
Description: Series statement: Prison of dreams ; book 5 | Originally published in Tamil as book five of a five book series under title: Kanavuc cirai. Oru putiya kālam. | Translated from the Tamil.

Identifiers: Canadiana (print) 20230590276 | Canadiana (ebook) 20230590284 | ISBN 9781774151242 (softcover) | ISBN 9781774151259 (EPUB) | ISBN 9781774151266 (PDF)

Subjects: LCGFT: Novels.
Classification: LCC PS8639.E93 K36413 2024 | DDC C894.8/113—dc23

Printed and bound in Canada by Coach House Printing

Mawenzi House Publishers Ltd.
39 Woburn Avenue (B)
Toronto, Ontario M5M 1K5
Canada

www.mawenzihouse.com

CONTENTS

Principal Characters

Abayan: Swarna's son with Uthayan.

Anil: an older Sinhala Leftist journalist who befriends Thiravi.

Chella: an elderly widow related to Arasi's late husband Velautham.

Gunananda (named Punchibanda at birth): a fundamentalist Bhuddhist monk obsessed with Swarna, and possibly responsible for her first husband Uthayan's death.

Gunarathnam (Gunam): Velupillai's older son.

Indran: Thambirasa's younger son, whom he now depends on to reverse the family's misfortune.

Kalan: (lit. Time), who is the attendant to the Yaman, the god of death.

Kanaka: a friend of Raji's in the refugee camp in Tamil Nadu.

Kanthsamy Nadaraja: also known as squint-eyed Nadaraja, the "scarecrow" who betrays Rakini to the military.

Kathirgesu: a teacher and master storyteller from a village in Jaffna, and the father of Prabu. He becomes a member of the executive council of the Tamil Cultural Assembly.

Kulasekaram: the husband of Thavamani, father of Siva, Vasanthi and Param, father-in-law of Mala.

Latchumidevi (Laxo): Pumani's daughter who joins the Movement and is killed.

Leela, Sheila, Mala: Saraswathi's older daughters.

Lek: Nesamalar's neighbour in Bangkok, and a sex worker. Traditionally, Lek is a masculine name.

Mahesh: Thambirasa's older son, who joins the Tigers as a sharpshooter.

Maheswari: a woman from Nainativu, who had moved there with her husband, the late Ponnusamy. She's the mother of Raji, Rajendran and Viji.

Manickavasagar: a social worker in Germany, who helps form the Tamil Cultural Assembly.

Manimekalai: the daughter of Swarna and Thiravi. She is named after the Tamil epic heroine from the Sangam period.

Mathavan: a young man from Trincomalee.

Mathi: an expert forger who works on the stolen or bought passports to smuggle people overseas.

Nagamma: Sankarapillai's wife and mother of Thiravi, Suganthi, Vaani and Nesan.

Nesamalar: a schoolteacher who is left stranded in India by a people trafficker.

Nimal Perera: a friend of Thiravi's, and a former JVP member who was forcibly disappeared by the military.

Ponnusamy: the late sub-postmaster in Nainativu, he was the husband of Maheswari.

Prabu: the son of Karthigesu, an educated young man who becomes a thug during his long separation from his family as he journeys West.

Pumani: Rajanayagam's daughter.

Puvanendran: Rakini's younger brother.

Rajakaruna: runs the pharmacy in the refugee camp in India, and helps train Raji to run the clinic.

Rajalakshmi (Raji): Maheswari's older daughter.

Rajanayagam: a retired Supreme Court Judge who seeks refuge in India after his home and family are ruined by the war.

Rajendran (Rajan): Maheswari's son, now an "agent" who helps smuggle Tamil people abroad with the help of his crew of forgers and thieves.

Rakini: a friend of Arasi's, and an experimental poet writing about the political situation.

Sankarananda Thero: the senior Buddhist monk at the Nagadipa Vihara.

Sankarapillai: Thiravi's father, a former teacher and politician.

Santhi: Thiravi's sister, who is disappeared and believed to be buried in Semmani.

Saraswathi: Viswalingam's wife, and mother of seven children.

Sellakili: a friend of Rakini's.

Sellathambu: a friend of Ponnusamy's.

Singaravelan/Singari: a thief who steals passports for the people smuggling crew led by Rajendran.

Sinthamani: a young woman who died when the boat she was in capsized in the sea.

Siva: a friend of Suthan and Thiravi's, colludes with the army and unsavoury rebel factions to transport goods into Jaffna.

Siva: a young man with a heart condition who had joined the Movement and been taken out of it by his father Kulasekaram. This Siva is married to Mala.

Sivanthan: Pumani's son who had killed himself following abuse in prison.

Sivasamy: also known as Sivasamithamilan (Tamil Sivasamy), an Indian Tamil self-respect activist who becomes sympathetic to the Movement.

Suntharalingam (Suntharam): a Tamil political activist.

Suthanthiran (Suthan): Suntharam's son.

Swarna: a Sinhala woman married to Uthayan.

Thambirasa: managed the lease on Maheswari's paddyfields, he is desperate for one of his sons to go overseas and return their family to a wealthy position.

Thamilarasi (Arasi): Suntharam's daughter.

Thangamma: the late Ponnusamy's sister.

Thavamani: wife of Kulasekaram and mother of Siva, mother-in-law of Mala.

Thayalan: Suthan's friend in Germany, married to Buvana.

Thiraviyam (Thiravi): Sankarapillai's older son, owner of the cooperative store.

Thisayan (Thisai): a former student of Thiravi's, an activist for the rights of hill country Tamils.

Thiyagu: a man with developmental disabilities, who was betrothed to Sinthamani.

Velayutham: Arasi's husband, a farmer. Killed by the army.

Valambikai: Suntharalingam's wife.

Velupillai: Maheswari's brother.

Vijayalakshmi (Viji): Maheswari's younger daughter, now married and settled in Canada.

Viswalingam: Saraswathi's husband, a man from Nainativu who has a gift for languages.

Vithuran: the child of Nesamalar and Malli, a thug who was expelled from the Movement.

Yogeswaran: Velupillai's younger son, who falls in love with Raji and joins the rebels with her encouragement.

2001

1

Chennai, India

THAT MORNING, THE LIGHT tore through the darkness and fog and fanned out around them. It had rained heavily the past two days. It had rained as though to swallow any hope of light returning. The radio forecasted forty-eight hours of storm and rain and warned fishermen not to take to the sea.

Mala had brought out some tea, saying, "What is this thundering pouring rain, maami? How do you think the meeting will end up?" Maheswari had no thought about it. Her care had shrunk and shrunk until it only encapsulated her family.

She had never really exceeded that boundary. She had not had the heart to leave Canada and come to India this time. She was too deeply wounded. She could never have imagined such a loss. He had gone to Canada at the end of ninety-nine, and before he had even spent a whole year there, he was gone forever. It seemed like it had happened in a fierce flash. Rajan had borrowed a friend's car one night. He had crashed into a truck on the highway, and the car was crushed; its tank caught fire and he had been burned to ashes. Was it possible that he had . . . fallen asleep? No, it was more likely he had been overwrought with emotion. It was only now she realized he had begun to drink so much in Canada because he had not been able to forget Amba.

How she had sheltered him as a child. She had sold her paddy plot for half its worth to send him to Bombay to get on a ship, to escape being recruited into some rebel group. She had been separated from him for fifteen years. Then, as soon she had the chance to see him and talk to him, she had snatched him from his wife and family and sent him to Canada. She hadn't been able to save him. Death had found him in the form of an accident. She cried till she was exhausted. This was the second death close to her. The first death in her home had been thirty years ago. It had shaken her to the core. This death destroyed the hopes of her womb. That wasn't all. It had cast her into a feeling of guilt that she was responsible for his death. It had been she who had destroyed his family, smashed it like a bird's nest. Silent as an insect, that Assamese girl had believed and accepted everything Maheswari had said and gone back to her village. Had her sins taken Rajan away from her? She thought about it over and over and shrank into herself.

The passage of time had given her some clarity. She had come half-heartedly for Raji's sake. She had hoped to coerce her. But, smug in having rescued her son, she had given Raji a window of time to come to a decision and gone back to Canada. The Assembly's anniversary had been scheduled for the previous year. They postponed it. She postponed her trip too. This time, as soon as the event was scheduled, her heart began to hope again, as of old. As soon as she heard that Suthan was going to India, she immediately planned for her travel. She left as soon as she got her visa.

She hadn't come here with any great purpose to send Raji off somehow with Suthan. She had decided that she would agree to her wishes. If she didn't go away with Suthan, she wanted to ask her if she would go with her to Canada. There was something more important too. It was about Amba. She had to let her know . . . she had secretly planned to accept Amba as her daughter-in-law and her son as a grandchild, and care for them. While she used to discuss all her plans with Viji, she kept this one so secret there was not even a hint of it outside. If everything worked out as she hoped, she thought she could work out the details later. Her heart longed to pick up the child and hug him. That was why she spoke about it to Viswalingam the day she arrived. It wasn't difficult for Viswalingam to go to Assam and return. He was just doubtful whether he could do anything with just the names Amba and Praba to go on, in a place where he didn't know the land or language. All the same, he went to Mumbai and asked the neighbours around their old house about them and got their descriptions, saying that he could use the information to search for them.

It was ten days since he left. He called once from Mumbai, and once from Assam. It had been three days since then. There had been no news after that. Assam was another state in a political crisis. If anything at all happened to him . . . The thought niggled at the back of her mind. In the last update, he had said, "I only have patchy information about where she might be. It's a small village far from the capital. I will leave tonight. The Vadapalani Murugan I have faith in won't let me down. I will return with the child and your daughter-in-law." Every time it rained in Chennai, Maheswari wondered if it rained in Assam; every time the wind blew, she wondered if it had caused any damage there.

Over and over the lightning flashed in the far distance. Over and over the thunder resounded. It was going to rain heavily, she thought, as she went to bed that night. But not a drop fell from the sky. At dawn, the fog dispersed in patches. The sun cast its rays in between. She lay on her bed in the room, looking out through the window. Kulathur was beautiful in that morning light. The pond had filled and brimmed wide as a lake. The mist still covered the lake. But it would disperse now. The hidden lushness would emerge.

Chandramohan was due to arrive at ten o'clock that morning. She didn't know if Suthan would come too. She had forgotten to ask. There was nothing unusual about that. She would speak normally to him and send him away. But she didn't want to see his ruined state yet again.

She had known him well in the village. From his childhood, he used to call her maami . . . maami whenever he saw her. When Suthan's family had moved to a different address she didn't see him as often. When she saw him later, she was surprised by how much he had grown. How tall . . . how strong . . . what a piercing gaze . . . and yet such humility. He would smile whenever he passed her. It had carried the weight of so many words. She had finally had the chance to see him again after so long. He was ruined. He stayed hunched as though he couldn't make himself stand upright. His face seemed permanently etched in pain, like a man who didn't know how to smile. It didn't seem he was conscious of anything apart from the Assembly.

Some of the wound in her was her pity for him.

She got up and prepared to have her bath.

When she heard that Mala had moved, she had wondered what the new house would be like. Though it was far from the Anna Nagar bus station, it had many luxuries, including its surroundings, spaciousness, and the air free from dust and smoke from vehicular traffic. It had been more than a year since Siva went to London. He had been accepted as a refugee there and sent them money every now and then. Now it was Mala who decided what kind of house to live in, where to find it and how much they could spend on the household in a month. In the past she would always ask Saraswathi: "Amma, what shall we do?" "Amma, can we do it this way?" Not anymore. Sheila also sent a little money for the family. But in one night, all the authority shifted to Mala.

It had happened the night that she got a phone call. "Mala . . . I have reached safely, Mala, no problems. I'm speaking to you from London now," Siva had said. The next day, at dawn, Mala sat in the middle of the room as if on a throne. When Saraswathi returned from washing her face, Mala said: "Why don't you all wake up a little earlier, amma? If we stay huddled under the sheets, dragging on until eight o'clock, the house will become a mess, won't it?" Viswalingam was listening from the verandah. Saraswathy made no protest. Viswalingam heard her quickly shake Poobathy, Thulasi, and the kids awake. Once the rush of rolling up mats had subsided, Saraswathi rushed out with the pot to get clean water from the water tank. She didn't look at Viswalingam. He could understand her feelings. For ten years, neither seated on a throne, nor as a queen, she had wielded a mother's authority. Now she had been overthrown. The little ones trailed behind Mala, saying Mala akka this, and Mala akka that. Senan was still an aimless loafer. But Mala gave him money for the cinema or for cigarettes whenever she wanted his support and kept him in her grip. Now whenever he left the house, he'd say "Akka . . . I'll be back soon." Poobathy was not here now. If she were, she would probably have gone the same way as Senan. Viswalingam had no concerns about any of this.

The children said goodbye to Mala when they left for school. They would go to the main street from there and take the bus.

When Maheswari returned from her bath, the tea Mala had set out for her had grown cold, so Mala heated it up and brought it back for her. That wasn't all, Mala felt indebted to do anything for Maheswari. Even if Maheswari refused help, Mala insisted. It was fitting for her to do so. Maheswari had rescued a shrivelled family. She had paid ten thousand dollars to an agent in London and arranged for Siva's journey herself. Sheila helped with the remainder, and Siva quickly reached London. Mala had dripped solicitude over Maheswari even when she had come to Chennai before.

She had hoped even then to melt maami's heart and somehow ask for her help. But that wasn't the only reason she had taken care of her. She had always been like that, even back home in the village. Whether to grind flour, to grind spices, to pound paddy—all Maheswari had to do was ask, and Mala would run over to help her. So did Saraswathi. They had done it expecting nothing in return.

Maheswari came out to the verandah with her teacup. She pulled out a chair and sat down.

The mist had lifted, and it was green everywhere.

She kept looking out.

"Would Viswalingam have found Amba?" she wondered.

Chandramohan arrived shortly after, in an auto. Arasi was with him. They pulled out chairs from the hall and sat outside. Chandramohan asked, "Is there any news from Viswalingam maama?"

"Not yet. That's what I think about all the time. Everyday, I keep hoping there'll be a phone call today or tomorrow."

Chandramohan could see that she had not emerged from her melancholy. He sensed that even though she said she believed Viswalingam would return safe and sound, she still had doubts. He hadn't failed to observe something else too. The last time he came, she had been fiercely determined that she would force Raji to consent to go to France. This time, no matter what she herself desired, she hadn't asked them to put any pressure on Raji. After what happened to the son she had forced to go along with her, she didn't seem likely to make any more decisions. He could see that was fair. But he couldn't go along with it. His friend's life took priority for him. So, he hesitantly said, "I don't feel like bringing up this issue urgently when you're in this state. But we are going to be leaving within a few days. If the anniversary celebrations begin on Friday, they'll be done by Sunday. My flight is next Wednesday.

Suthan will be leaving around that time too. So, we need to find out what Raji wants very quickly. It doesn't matter what it is. After that, Suthan and I won't even think about this anymore. You can trust me on this."

This meant that they had come to a resolution. It was she who lacked resolve. If Viswalingam came back from Assam with a positive answer, she'd feel half strengthened. But at the moment she couldn't say anything. Though she had the authority to make a decision, she was afraid to take a firm stance on anything after Rajendran died. Even the thought of him made her tremble. It felt as if her nerves were dead, and her blood flowed more slowly. But she had to tell them Raji's answer once the conference was over. "Okay, thambi," she said, looking at Chandramohan.

Mala returned from the market. It was obvious from her face, when she opened the door, that she had news. "Thiraviyam annai is coming on Friday morning," she said.

"How do you know?" Arasi asked.

"The judge told me."

Did Arasi's face show any reaction to the news? Not enough to be visible. But her heart was filled with all kinds of strange emotions. When waves drift away from the shore, they sometimes climb and leap over waves coming in. Her heart seemed to play back and forth in such a manner. Her desire told her that all was not over yet. Sometimes, she woke up before dawn. Velayutham was gone. Many of her memories of him had faded too. Even when they returned to her, they didn't overwhelm her as they once did. It was the result of her recreating herself as a new woman in a new arena. But the desire he had stirred in her had not left yet. She had made it the subject of one her poems, titled "Refusal."

It was ten o'clock when Chandramohan left. Arasi left with him, saying she would return another day.

2

Chennai, India

ON THE DAY OF the conference, Maheswari, Raji, and Arasi had been wandering on Ranganathan Road following their lunch. Maheswari bought a few things. As they prepared to catch an auto to leave, Arasi told them she would walk to the festivities.

It was then that she caught sight of two young men. Just as she was thinking that they looked familiar, they walked over to the pedestrian crossing. From behind, one of them looked just live Puvanendi. She knew the tall boy next to him, too. Could it be Yogesh . . . here? They had crossed the street and she tried calling after them, "Thambi . . . ?"

The traffic had picked up after the afternoon lull, and now it prevented her attempts to reach them.

As she walked to the festival, her mind was restless. It was Puvanendi and Yogesh. She was quite sure of it now.

The day's events ended by seven-thirty. There were fewer people at the afternoon sessions. Even they had begun to disperse when they saw the sky darkening. The remaining few scrambled to leave as soon as the sessions were done.

Despite the light drizzle and the cool caress of the breeze, Arasi kept talking animatedly with Raji. It felt as though no one could say anything meaningful that day. Though she made some observations here and there, she was puzzled to realize that she had swept them all aside to think about later.

Thiraviyam was speaking to someone off to a side. Suthan was off to another side speaking to Canada Selvarajah. Even as he talked, he was waiting for Thiravi. It looked as though Thiravi was dragging on his conversation with that stranger. She wasn't sure whether it was because he wanted Suthan to come up to him, or because he wanted to prevent Suthan from approaching him. The mystery was solved shortly after. When Suthan turned away for a while and turned back, Thiravi had disappeared.

Some thirty odd years ago, friends and family who lived far from each other were united in the micro-island of Katchatheevu. Separated in two countries, they used the lassitude in border security granted during the Katchatheevu Church Festival to meet and celebrate on the island.

It seemed that Suthan's hope that this soil would be a meeting place between friends who now lived in the Western world and in Sri Lanka had proved false. The thought tugged at his heart. Suthan had understood his nature even from childhood. Yet, he found it hard to bear. He had gone astray just once, when the beliefs and activities of the different Movements had not been clearly defined. As though in punishment for it, he had been wounded in his left leg. He used his limp to remind himself of his unforgettable, irrevocable mistake. Then he had suffered for six months when he was injured in the shoulder in Germany in ninety-nine. That was when Prabu had died beside him.

Didn't events inspire any pity for him?

Arasi's eyes fixed on him from directly across the hall. Was she watching his disappointment? She snapped her head in the other direction when he saw her. She walked up to Rajanayagam, who was standing in the entrance as though expecting someone and began talking to him.

Suthan understood her frame of mind. She didn't seem to be affected much by Thiravi's departure. His friend's rejection was only a great sorrow to him.

3

Chennai, India

MALA HAD BEEN WATCHING Maheswari for a long time as
she paced in her room, stepped into the hall, and walked up to the
entrance and then went back to her room and sat on her bed, lost
in thought. She felt very sorry for her. How much more tired she
looked. She knew Maheswari was watching for her father every
minute. More than anticipating his arrival, she seemed to long
for it. Mala knew that Maheswari hadn't recovered from the loss
of Rajendran. She had gathered it from the few times Maheswari
had talked about him. Once she said, "If I had let him join the
Movement and he had died in battle . . . or at least died here while
he was with his wife and child . . . it wouldn't have hit me so hard,
Mala. I kept him sheltered for so long. And finally . . . "

There was some justice in her sorrow. But Maheswari was part
of a community that seemed to see and hear of death so cheaply
now, Mala couldn't understand why she was so distraught. But
death shakes every community, even if only at that moment.
Death is unique in that there is no person who doesn't tremble
at it.

Maheswari could see that Mala was watching her. She realized that Mala was staying awake because of her. She knew that she was also thinking as she waited for her. Just like her, Mala had many problems, even if they were small ones. The whole family was full of problems.

At first there was only a conflict between Saraswathi and Viswalingam. Now there were conflicts inside each of them.

Within a few days of arriving, she realized that there was even a conflict between Mala and her mother. But she made nothing of it. It was natural to have fights within a family. Sometimes the fights were a sign of a deep love. Maheswari knew that.

She was only puzzled about Poobathy. When she first came and asked them about her, mother and daughter said she was in Trichy. Senan said nothing. Viswalingam was not there at the time. She thought she would get the truth from Viswalingam. But she wondered why she should have to pry so much to learn about the matter and let it go.

Maheswari got up and turned off the light. A short while after she lay down, she heard someone call "Mathi" from the entrance.

Mathi was the youngest child. When Mala went to open the door, Viswalingam walked in. He lit the lamp in the hall.

Maheswari hurried out.

Saraswathi followed.

Viswalingam went straight to the bathroom, He washed his face, hands, and feet and came out. He wiped himself with a towel. The lines of his ribs stood out in stripes on his body and spoke of his wanderings.

He sat across from them and exhaled as though to calm his emotions. He bent and kept shaking his head. Then he sat up and spoke: "I have committed some crime in another life, thangachi. It's the worst misery that can befall a person. Or I wouldn't have had to see or speak of it myself."

"What happened there, annai?" Maheswari asked.

"What happens? I saw Amba. And when she heard what had happened to Rajendran, how that child cried . . . ah God, no one should face this torment. She must have thought I had come to bring her back, or that I had brought her some news about Rajan . . . she saw me at a distance and how she came running carrying the child . . . "

Viswalingam wept. The man seemed to be slightly drunk. If he hadn't been, he would have exploded. He composed himself and went on: "I didn't know how to tell her. Then, somehow . . . I had to tell her, didn't I? Isn't that why I went? I told her. When I told her it looked like she fell dead to the floor. I thought I should have died along the way rather than see such a thing."

Maheswari noticed that he didn't mention he had gone along with her as if to help in separating them. But she knew it didn't mean he wasn't thinking about it.

"Then?"

"What then? We calmed down, somehow."

"Mm."

"She asked if a rebel group had done this. I told her no, that it was an accident. When I told her you had asked me to bring them back, she started crying again. I told her you wouldn't have done this if you didn't have a strong reason, and finally got her to agree to come."

"Go on, annai."

"'I'll come, but not today . . . I'll come when I have recovered a little. I'll come within two or three weeks,' that's what she said."

"You should have stayed back and brought her with you . . . "

"I asked her. She said the situation in the village was not good. 'Go, tell maami,' she said, and sent me away."

He rose, having said all he had to say. Seeing Maheswari sitting there still, he said: "I didn't think she was saying it just to get rid of me . . . she will come."

It was only when he turned back that he saw Saraswathi, still seated, leaning against the door. He couldn't hide the amazement in his face.

He went into the room and brought out his mat. He dropped it down with a thump and kicked it open with his foot.

Mala didn't stay any longer. Maheswari got up after a while and went to her room too.

When she went to bed, her mind felt somewhat at peace.

She had held her first grandchild. But now she felt a longing for her son's child. She would think of the child as if it was him.

As she drifted off to sleep, she heard voices in the hall. It sounded like Saraswathi. "Saraswathi? And Viswalingam?"—even as she thought this, the darkness closed into her mind.

When she woke up at dawn, the same thought continued in her mind. She couldn't understand what had happened here. They hadn't moved closer out of any need. A distance grown in one place had turned into a closeness in another place.

Maheswari had realized as soon as she arrived that Saraswathi was no longer in the same position that she had been two years before. She had no place to go and was stuck there, from one day to the next. Her pride in her own household had been crushed, and a distance had grown between her and Mala. It was always possible that the authority would shift to Mala once Siva went abroad. Money decides dominance, and that is true of authority in the family. It was Mala who stayed in touch with Sheila. She had spoken of her as a curse, but suddenly she became her precious thangachi. It was Mala who shared any news about Sheila. Even when they got their own telephone, it remained under her domain. If there was any phone call when she was away, she wanted to know all the details, even if it hadn't been for her. It was unavoidable that Saraswathi would be pushed into second place under these conditions. The distance that had grown between Saraswathi and Mala had turned into a closeness between Saraswathy and Viswalingam.

Maheswari was able to figure out the core issue that had given shape to this shift.

4

Chennai, India

YOGESH HAD CLIMBED HALFWAY up the stairs to the balcony and sat staring into the distance.

The sky was growing dark. It looked as though it dissolved and flowed. But he wasn't paying attention to the sky.

As the scent trapped within the petals is released when the sun tears through the earth and climbs the sky, he only realized how much love he had in his heart for her in the beating of his heart at the thought of seeing her again. It was not a thought; it was something different. Longing. A longing for life.

He didn't know if he could see her again. Even if he arranged for it, even if he didn't speak to her but created an opportunity to take a long look at her, Mulla wouldn't allow it.

The five women he had seen that afternoon at the fabric shop on Ranganathan Road were all known to him. One of them was his father's own sister. Yet, he could not say a word to them. Mulla was a grinding mortar stone around his neck.

Mulla was lying down inside. He must have fallen asleep by now. He was a rebel as well. He lived by rules and regulations. He didn't know the meaning of tenderness. He didn't know how to ease off. When Yogesh had tried to leave for the Cultural Assembly sessions that morning, saying he'd like to check it out, Mulla had stopped him, saying he couldn't. They had stood in the doorway, their conversation getting heated.

"It's not my job to listen to what you say. The leadership asked me to bring you here: I did. Once you've done what you came to do, let me know and I'll deliver you back. My job ends there," Yogesh had yelled at him.

Mulla had stood for a moment in shock, his eyes welling with tears. "You will get in trouble if I go back, Yogesh. That's why I stopped you," he said.

Yogesh understood his concerns. But something within him made him want to provoke the boy. It was a pull that affected his heart . . . his life . . . How would this man know? But he tried his best to pacify him, saying, "I know Chennai very well, Mulla. Don't worry about anything. I'll just go look around and be back."

"Then I'm coming too," Mulla said.

"And leave no one at the house? Are we going to lock it up?" To which Mulla replied, "Gunalan said he'll come by in the evening." If Gunalan came by and had to turn back, it would create unnecessary delays, Yogesh thought, and said they could wait until Sivasithambaram returned and let him know before they left.

It was eleven by the time they both left for Pandi Bazaar. It was only after he had got out at Thiyagaraya Nagar, walked along Station View Road, and floated into Ranganathan Road, that the group of women, standing by themselves in the afternoon sun, caught his eye. He was taken aback at the sight of his maami. Then Arasi, Kamala, and only then did he recognize Raji.

He stood watching her for five minutes. Then Mulla said, "Let's go get some tea." When they returned, the women were nowhere to be seen. He ran to the main road. He had wondered in surprise that Mulla had not tried to stop him. What was even more surprising was that he too seemed to look at one of them as though she was someone he cared about.

Yogesh decided he didn't need to go to the conference anymore. He was happy with what he had seen on the way.

As soon as they got back, Sivasithambaram asked, "How was the conference, thambi?"

Mulla replied, "It was good. But it was very crowded. So we left."

Sivasithambaram went on talking. Mulla was trapped. Yogesh tactfully slipped away. But he could overhear their conversation.

"What is your agent saying?"

They had been told that the man had been in a camp, that they should pay an agency and wait to arrange for him to go overseas. Neither Mulla nor Yogesh knew him directly. Yogesh had found an old friend when they arrived on the Nagapatnam shore in Tamil Nadu and got the letter. They had only asked for a place to stay until they found a safe house.

Mulla said something in reply and appeased Sivasithambaram. Then he asked, "What's happening with the house?"

"We'll find out tomorrow. Never mind that, aiyya, did anyone come in search of us while we were out?"

"No, thambi. Was someone coming about the house?"

"Yes."

Gunalan had not arrived by ten o'clock. "It'll be tomorrow, then. He'll come with good news for sure," Mulla said, even before Yogesh asked.

After dinner, Mulla spread out his mat and fell asleep immediately.

Yogesh hadn't known Mulla at all back home. He had never seen him. One day the head of the division called Yogesh over, and Mulla was there. The head had said, "Yogesh, we need to take him to India and bring him back."

"Can be done."

"What's the situation like?"

"It's a little tough. But the boats are still going out with refugees even now."

"The refugees are another issue. Even if they get dropped off on a sandspit, the Indian navy will pick them up and drop them off on the shore somewhere. Even if they get caught, the worst that can happen is the boat is confiscated. But if you get caught . . . "

"We won't get caught," Yogesh said.

Mulla stood staring at him, in awe at his certainty.

The division head turned to Mulla: "We're sending a very skilled boatman with you. I wouldn't do such a favour for just anyone. The higher ups have told me to, so I must do it. You need to finish what you're doing in a couple of days and get back here by day five, day six. If you need any help over there, Yogesh can get it done. Be careful on your mission. Don't get caught by the Indian police or the Sri Lankan navy under any circumstances."

Even after he took him aboard and brought him across, he hadn't known the mission Mulla had come to carry out. Even after they arrived, and he knew what it was, he didn't know who he was, how he was going to do it, or even why. His rigid face wouldn't brook any questions. He had the focus of a man who had come to take out a traitor. Anyhow, Gunalan would come the next day with some definite news. They would get the job done the next day or the day after and it would be time to leave.

It was almost twelve o'clock.

He could hear the sound of the ocean.

There was a beautiful beach in this part of Besant Nagar. He had roamed that area for a few days some time ago.

The sea always seemed linked to him somehow. Even now, the sound it made, seemed to communicate with him somehow. Life's events are not only linked to times, but also to the special characteristics of places.

It took him a long time to fall asleep that night.

5

Chennai, India

AFTER HE GOT OUT at Egmore station, crossed the road and walked down the alley to the lodge, Thiravi remembered that Arasi had told him her brother might come to meet him that day. He looked around the entrance and the reception to see if Suthan was there when he walked in. He ate the food he had brought with him and went to bed immediately.

He had flown from Colombo to Trivandrum, then got on a bus traveling through the night to Chennai and rushed out to the conference venue as soon as he got there. His body was begging for some rest. Even as he wondered about Suthan, he fell into a deep net of slumber.

Suddenly he heard knocking on the door. He woke up, completely disoriented, unconscious of east and west, place or time and lay with his eyes open for a while. It was a kind of fear. It was a sign of living in a country where anything could happen at any time. He had been woken by a knocking on his door in the middle of the night or in the early hours of the morning many times now. He had escaped unscathed, somehow. Except for this fear . . . when there was a knock at the door, and when he awoke.

After a few moments of confusion, it all came back to him. When he remembered that Arasi had told him Suthan would come to his room somehow, he lay there for a while, without the will to get up. He reluctantly rose and opened the door.

The lodge manager stood outside. Behind him, Suthan.

"He said it was very urgent, he needs to see you," the man said.

"Hm." Thiravi grunted and looked at Suthan. "Come in," he said.

They were meeting face to face after many years. When they had been such close friends. That was when the conch store had been a gathering place. There had been days when he had worried at not seeing him. How had they come to this point where they hesitated with each other, even when within arm's reach?

"Sit."

Suthan sat on the bed.

He knew it must have been hard for him to get into the lodge from the way the manager had knocked at his door. "What is it?" he asked.

Some of his qualities had not changed at all, Thiravi thought. He bent his head, just as he used to. It was a sign of some guilt. Thiravi knew it wouldn't be easy to bring him out of it. He bent low and looked into Suthan's face. What was going on? Why were his eyes glistening? Were those tears in his eyes? It was always Suthan who calmed and resolved a conflict. But now he was silent, as though labouring under a terrible confusion.

How long would it take for him to calm himself?

It grew quiet outside.

"Tell me why you're here. I need to wake up early. I have a thousand tasks to finish while I'm here," Thiravi said.

Instead of a reply, silence filled the room. The fan swirled above them, faintly disturbing the quiet.

Seeing him struggle, Thiravi relented a little. "Tell me, what's going on? What can we do if you don't talk?"

It was true. He had come here to say something. He had to spit it out without thinking about the consequences. Before the fatigue and hesitation took him over again, "I've failed," Suthan said, coming to himself.

Thiravi looked at him without speaking.

"The only thing I can salvage anymore is my friendship."

"You must have thought you would succeed, isn't that so? We're all idiots. We don't know anything. You're the only clever one. So, you didn't talk to anyone about it . . . you decided on your own, you idiot! And now you've lost everything you had."

Suthan was a defensive person. He could be incredibly hardheaded. But now, he seemed silent, as if in assent.

Thiravi continued, "If all this had happened to you some other way, I would have been the first to feel sorry for you, even before anyone in your family. There are too many people who have lost their spouses in our country. You should feel sorry for all of them. That's why there's a quickly growing culture of people living together now, rather than getting married. That's how we're coping with the losses we face. It's a good, sacred thing. It's the great tragedy of a warring nation that human life is snatched from us. There's no place on earth where it became as cheap as in our country. My life has been ruined too. But I haven't ruined lives like you have."

After a pause, he went on, "Do whatever you want. We're not children anymore. We need to think about many things and understand them and figure out what to do, you . . . you did whatever you wanted, and have fallen apart. The most I can do for you now is to hope that nobody else ever goes through this, and to feel sorry for you. Okay . . . okay . . . it's one-thirty—here's a pillow and a bedsheet, spread it out and sleep. I don't think you need to go out now. But it's up to you."

Suthan took the pillow and bedsheet and put them on the floor.

The two of them went to sleep.

Though there was no streetlamp outside, a yellow light spilled in through the glass window facing the street.

"Thiraviyam!"

"What?"

"Just one thing ... will you believe me if I tell you?"

"Tell me."

"There's just one mistake that's at the root of all my mistakes."

"That you suddenly joined the Movement?"

"Mm. But I didn't make that original mistake on my own ... "

"Then?"

"A circumstance ... a circumstance that I couldn't avoid came up and ... "

"Don't lie. You had links with the Movement even when you were on campus."

"I'm not denying that. Back then, the Movement was all the groups involved in the struggle. It was a time of questions. A lot of people didn't feel the struggle would succeed. Still . . . after the eighty-three riots, everyone felt the need. I felt it too. But my family situation wouldn't easily allow me to join a rebel group. I was struggling with this, when ... "

"Oh!"

"The second day after I left on the boat, I came back. I tried so hard to tell Raji at least. I saw her but couldn't bring myself to say anything. I stayed quiet. And then? I just got sent on to training."

"A lot has happened since then too ... "

"That's when we hit the Akkaraipatru bank. That was the day I first thought of leaving the Movement. But after that, all kinds of things happened, and it ended up like this ... "

Thiravi stayed silent.

Time moved quickly toward dawn. It was the time when the city slept.

Thiravi felt he could think more about Suthan now. He had got caught up in his passion and taken part in some Movement activities, then unavoidably got pulled into training and become a rebel, found himself unable to commit to it and escaped, got into illegal activity, went to Europe . . . things followed one after the other. The consequences of one mistake, just as he said. His wedding, his relationship with Sheila . . . all these mistakes had erupted from that first root mistake. He had come to regret his mistakes. Hence his fervent activity with the Assembly. He thought Suthan's friend Chandramohan must be a great support to him in all this.

Thiravi decided that he shouldn't be too hasty when it came to Suthan. Pain was a sign of rot.

Suthan was immersed in thought too. He was amazed that Thiravi knew all these things . . . When he awoke in the morning, he washed his face, in a hurry to get to his hotel in Purasaiwakkam. As he turned to say goodbye, Thiravi, who had woken up but was still lying in bed, asked, "Does the injury in your shoulder still hurt you?"

"Just a little."

Suthan felt as though his heart had grown a little lighter.

6

Chennai, India

AS SHE CAUGHT A bus to leave Valluvar Kottam, Arasi felt a deep loneliness, as though she were leaving a spouse behind. Could she feel so deeply after just a short time spent in his company? That evening told her she could.

She had gone on long journeys alone before. She had never known a feeling of loneliness to overwhelm her then, why did it do so now, when she'd left him behind in Valluvar Kottam?

It was true that he had always been a kind of masculine ideal for her.

After she had accidentally bumped into him in Thunukkai once, whenever she went to Colombo she had hoped to see him again. She had waited many days. When she saw him, just before she left for India, and walked along the beach with him, the sensation of brushing against his skin had stayed in her mind as a pleasant memory.

How excited Arasi had got the day Mala said Thiravi was coming from Colombo!

These were all signs of a strong feeling, weren't they?

Another thought occurred to her then. Was she thinking of

giving up her hermit life, where she carried out her own duties in the struggle? The letter she wrote Suthan when he was in Germany had been important to her. Her reply to him was still carved in stone in her mind.

He tried to stop violence against a daughter of this land and died as a witness to the atrocities committed on the Tamil people. People like me must safeguard the memory of that witnessing and live on here. It is not our fate; it is a duty—a contribution.

Did her desires oppose that duty? She now had a reputation as a poet. Words held value for her. Not only the spoken word, but also the words in her mind. Could she remain indifferent? She couldn't. But time was changing it. No one can fully ignore the compulsion of time. Not even a poet.

Her duty to the nation was important too. It was true she had hoped to live as a witness. But it's a trial that needs a witness, why a witness to war? It was a kind of penance to live on in that land with a commitment to an ideal. She only had the page that time had put in her hand. She still hadn't seen what was written on it.

A grandmother who lived next door to her used to say that her fate had been written scratch by scratch with stone. Was that how it would be for her too? Or would it be written with a golden needle, to suit her?

As the fluttering of her mind calmed, she thought about why she hadn't told him about Yogesh and Puvanendi. It wasn't that she had forgotten. She had deliberately not told him. Though she had thought about it the whole evening, she couldn't be sure it was Yogesh. It was the same with Puvanendi. She didn't know how she could say she had seen two men who looked like Yogesh and Puvanendi, so she didn't bring it up.

The bus reached the Anna Nagar roundabout. Arasi got out. The drizzle had stopped. Now she needed to take a bus to Ayanavaram. That's when it happened.

In an auto turning away from Anna Nagar, she saw the men who looked like Yogesh and Puvanendi.

Arasi could not settle down when she went home. She went to a phone booth across the street and called Raji. If it was Yogesh, there was a chance he had met with Raji.

"Raji!"

"Who is it, Arasi? Yes, speak."

"When I left you all in the afternoon . . . "

"Yes . . . "

"I saw . . . two people . . . they were a little far away. One looked exactly like our Yogesh. The boy who was with him also looked like a boy I know, Raji."

"Like Yogesh?"

"Yes. I couldn't be sure at first. That's why I didn't say anything about it to you or to Thiraviyam. Then around nine o'clock this morning when the bus was stuck at the Anna Nagar roundabout, I saw the same two in an auto. If it was Yogesh, I thought he might try to come and see you . . . "

"He didn't, Arasi."

She had no more to say.

Was Raji in shock? Arasi felt terrible that she had unnecessarily brought up her suspicions and upset her. She quickly tried to think of something else. "I think Suthan will somehow go and see Thiraviyam today," she said.

"How do you know?"

She told her that she had seem him ask Rajanayagam for his address.

7

Chennai, India

WHEN SHE HEARD THE knocking at the door, Raji opened her eyes irritated, as if she had just fallen asleep. Seeing the bright beams of sunlight pouring through the window she realized it was well past dawn.

It had been past two when she went to bed last night. Kamala had said her eyelids were drooping and went to bed at around midnight. Raji sat alone in the hall. A Hindi film was playing on the television with the volume on low, and there was a fight scene on.

She had been confused beyond thinking.

Just like Arasi, she couldn't believe that Yogesh had come to Chennai. But later, she believed it. She believed it because it was Yogesh. She was worried he might even come to the house.

He was a rough man. Uneducated. But he was well-mannered. Though she was afraid that he might come, she felt herself increasingly wishing that he would. Feelings don't become numb at that age. Even when life cruelly weighs a human being down with problems, these emotions sometimes break free from their restraints and roar.

Then a thought rose in her mind that shattered all those

feelings. He would have become a fighter now. Another fighter had come with him. Why would they come here at a time when the Assembly was holding its conference? Was it to carry out some frightful mission? Or perhaps . . . was this to harm Suthan directly? Was it possible that he too had been a target in the shooting in Germany, and he had escaped? There was no evidence of one thing or another and this seemed the most likely.

The situation made her worry for her mother as well. Though she mourned her brother too, her mother had lost someone who would have lit her funeral pyre, and she bore the greater sorrow. All these thoughts roiled in Raji's mind. She couldn't remember how she had stood up and turned off the television and gone to lie down.

When she opened the door, Kamala asked: "Did you stay awake for a long time, Raji?"

Raji, her reddened eyes blinded by the light, squinted to look at her and smiled wanly.

"Okay, go wash your face and come. Someone has come from Trichy . . . " Kamala said and moved aside.

Raji washed her face and came into the hall; there was no one there. She rushed out eagerly. Thiyagu sat hunched in the front yard.

She was amazed. What relationship did she have with him? What affection wove him to her? They were from the same village, that was all. It had nothing to do with him knowing Suthan. There was a deep affection. And a wide one. He was loving for the sake of being loving, with no expectation of anything in return. He made himself a slave to love.

"What is it, Thiyagu? When did you come?" Raji asked.

"I came yesterday. When I got here the gate was locked. I came by five times and looked. The gate didn't open. I asked everyone where you had gone . . . that house . . . this house . . . the house next door. Finally, finally someone told me you had gone out in the morning. Where did you go?"

"Never mind that, you could have come in the evening?"

"I fell asleep."

"Where?"

"At Veerabaku's house."

"At Veerabaku's house? How do you know him?"

"I met him at a shop. He's from Ceylon also! When I told him I had come from the camp, he asked me to come for dinner and asked me to stay."

"Okay. Why did you come from the camp in a hurry? Did you tell them you were leaving? Or did you leave secretly?"

"I didn't tell them I was leaving."

"Mm. Who gave you money for your ticket?"

"There are some single boys at the camp, no?"

"Yes . . . "

"I take water to them . . . wash their shirts . . . they give me money. I gave it to maami to save for me. I took money out of that."

"Which maami?"

"Nagamma maami, only."

"Malar's mother?"

"Who else?"

"Mm. But why did you take so much trouble to come here? Didn't I write to you, saying I'll come soon?"

"When did you write?"

"Didn't I reply to your postcard?"

"That? That was six months ago."

She was mildly taken aback. Had it been that long? She had forgotten all about it. She had no plans to go back there, now. Even after Valambikai came over, she occasionally used to go to Trichy to see Malar or Ganesalingam. Malar had got married, got her visa, and moved to Norway. Ganesalingam's daughter who used to live in Pondicherry, moved to London and took her parents there as well. She had not had a need to go to Trichy after that. In a way, she had lied to Thiyagu in her letter.

"Okay. Why have you come to see me in such a hurry?"

"Just wanted to."

"Hm. Then talk away."

"What to say . . . mm . . . did Suthan's mother go to Nainativu?"

"No. She's here in Chennai."

"Here?"

"Do you know Suthan's akka?"

"Yes . . . very well. Isn't she the girl who got blisters on the side of her mouth from mango sap?"

"How long ago was that? Yes, her. She's here with her mother too."

"I would like to see them."

"Wait a while. You can see everyone. Even your friend Suthan."

"Even Suthan?" Thiyagu's whole face blossomed. "Can I see him here? Suthan came from abroad?"

"He's here."

"I want to see Suthan now! Raji . . . Raji . . . tell me where he is, I'll go myself and see him."

She knew he would give her trouble and she still told him. He had stepped into the deadly strait and swum here to see Suthan. She said, "Suthan is in the hotel. We can't go and see him there."

"Will he come to his mother's house?"

"Mm . . . that's when we can see him. Okay, when are you going back?"

"Where, to the island?"

"No, to the camp."

"I won't go to the camp anymore."

"It's hard to stay here."

"I will stay with Veerabaku."

"It'll be hard for you to stay there, too. If you're going to stay outside, you must register with the police here."

"If I don't register, will they catch me and take me?"

"Mm . . ."

He thought about it. She could tell from his face that he was deeply upset. Then he asked: "What will they do if they catch me?"

"They'll send you back home."

" . . . "

"Why, don't you want to go back home?"

"I want to see Suthan!"

"Will you go back after you see Suthan?"

"After that, I want to see Sinthamani!"

"Just say that you don't want to go back to the village."

"No . . . after I see everyone . . . I can go back to the village with Sinthamani."

There was a decisiveness in his words which there had never been before.

Kamal brought them some tea. Thiyagu drank it. Then, "If Suthan comes to his mother's house, will you let me know?" he asked.

She said she would.

"When will he come?"

She said he would come soon.

Thiyagu said he would stay at Veerabaku's place until then and left.

8

Chennai, India

AN INEXPLICABLE ECSTASY HAD taken over Thiravi's heart that morning.

At dawn he felt a sweet breeze and heard sweet sounds.

But the ecstasy was not because of these.

Perhaps . . . ecstasy cannot be explained?

Something grew in his mind that was neither dream nor reality but healed his heart.

It was early morning, he remembered. Sankarananda had appeared to him. He was tired. He had a white stubble on his head and his chin. It looked like he had walked far. Sweat, dust, dirt, fatigue covered his body. His teeth were rotting. Behind his preaching lips his mouth was dark where his teeth had fallen out.

But his eyes kept flashing . . . flashing with a glow. His gaze held and embraced him, comforting him.

"Ah!" The monk said in relief. "How far! How many days!"

"Why, bhikkhu?"

"In search of you."

"In search of me? Why, bhikkhu?"

He looked out across the expanse and gazed at the sky, as

though he had much on his mind. Then he smiled lightly. "You really don't know why I've been searching for you? Oh!"

The silence lengthened between them until he broke it, with: "The Walawwa Gana monk searched for me. I searched for you. I have not even nurtured a quarter of the wisdom he planted in me to share with anything else. I would have been satisfied that I had shared at least half my wisdom with humanity, especially the children of this soil, if my historical tract had been published. But Gunananda and his gang have destroyed all my efforts."

"Yes, Thero. Anil aiyya escaped with his life very narrowly that day. But we were able to save some of the pages of your great history from the beginning and the end."

"Yes."

"They are safe with me."

"I know. That is why I have come in search of you."

"Thero!"

"Yes, Thiravi. I've come in search of you now for those pages."

"I'll give them to you, Thero."

"I didn't come in search of you to get those pages back. It was so that humanity receives their meaning. They hold the solution to a problem. They are life guides to the Sinhalese and the Tamils. Make them speak to the Sinhalese and the Tamils. They are not meant to sleep, but to speak. They must come out as the sermons left behind by the preaching bhikkhu. Will you do this?"

Thiravi hesitated.

"You can do it. Will you?"

"I will."

"May you be graced by Lord Buddha."

The blessing descended on him like a waterfall.

Thero!

He awoke in ecstasy.

Now he could not sleep. Not only because the responsibility

had been placed on him, but because it had dawned.

He sat up on his bed, feeling a second ecstasy as he thought for a while in perfect calm about all he could do to fulfill this responsibility.

Whether it was dream or reality, it was an experience. He had immersed himself in the Jataka tales and the tales of Buddha throughout his childhood. The ideals of Buddhism had delighted him even at that young age. He had never had a dream like this. Yet he didn't feel very surprised when it happened.

He hadn't neglected the remnants of the tract that survived the blaze; even before the dream he desired them to be of some use. But he hadn't known what to do with them.

But now the bhikkhu himself had shown him the way.

The festival was a good time to help spread the bhikkhu's message to the right people. He had brought copies of the pages with him. But they were in Sinhala. They needed to be translated. It would be wonderful if someone could do it quickly. But who?

Someone from the lodge came to tell him he had a phone call. He got up and went with him. It was Rajanayagam. "Can you drop by here on your way to the festival, Thiraviyam?"

"Okay."

It was eight o'clock when he got to Rajanayagam's house. When he went in, he saw the reverend Brother James seated there. "Aren't you coming to the festival today?" he asked.

"My stomach is upset. I couldn't sleep at all last night. I might need to get some medicine for it," James said.

It was only after they began talking that he realized that Rajanayagam had called him at James's request. Before he could speculate why, James came straight to the point. He told him he wanted to speak to him about the bhikkhu Sankarananda. "Did you know him personally?"

"I did."

"Did you know him very well?"

"I couldn't say that. He used to oversee the Naga Vihara in Nainativu for a long time. I didn't see him for more than ten years after the riots. Then he suddenly came in search of me, to my house."

"Why?"

Thiravi held back his answer. He needed to know why he was being asked these questions.

Rajanayagam understood his reticence and explained. James had come to know a little about Sankarananda through the newspapers. At first, he had thought the stories were part of the government's propaganda. But the previous night the monk had come up in conversation again, for some reason. Rajanayagam told him that Thiravi might know something about him. James wanted to call him that morning, to ask him what he knew of the monk.

Thiraviyam remained expressionless. His mind was focused on Sankarananda. Hadn't he just had a remarkable vision early that morning? Now, when he woke up, someone else was calling him to speak about the same man.

Wonders do happen.

He was surprised by James.

He looked like a priest he had seen in a French film. He spoke wisely and quietly. But his opinions and his words were strong as nails. He seemed to speak with a clarity of intent.

"Thiraviyam!" Rajanayagam interrupted his reverie. "James wants to know about the history book the bhikkhu was writing."

"Oh," Thiravi laughed, realizing his inattention must have seemed rude. "It was all destroyed when some thugs vandalized and burned down the Seven Seas office."

"It's all burned?!" James's voice gave away the depth of his disappointment. "I asked because I wanted to know more about it. Can you tell us how, and with what intention he had written it?"

Thiraviyam explained the gist of it from what he had heard from Anil.

"Is there such a bhikkhu? I can't believe it! I had thought all these days that the Buddhists and Muslims hadn't made any efforts towards reconciliation, the way the Lankan parish priests, and other priests had done," James said.

"If his book had been published, it would have been a great opportunity for the Sinhalese to understand themselves. Anil told me there was a lot in there for Tamils to think about too. It's all ruined. Well . . . I have a few pages remaining. There is a chance that we can work out the direction of the book as a whole."

"Some pages didn't get burnt?"

Thiraviyam nodded.

"You have them?"

"I do. I have a xerox copy."

"Do you have it here? Can I see it?"

"It's in Sinhala."

"Give it to me, I know Sinhala."

Thiravi opened his bag, took out the copy and handed it over. The Brother took it from him and remained perfectly still for ten minutes as he read. Then he asked, "Do you know what's written here?"

Thiravi said he didn't.

His excitement unabated, James said animatedly, "This message should be shared with the world, Thiraviyam."

Thiravi thought about his dream. How strange that everything was falling into place on its own. "Do you think you can reconstruct some of the ideas based on the beginning and end passages you have there?" he asked.

"I certainly can. With a small introduction and a short explanation, it can be published as a slim volume."

"Can you do that? I have to leave next week."

"I can definitely do that."

Thiravi's joy knew no bounds.

Suddenly James remembered something. "One more thing . . . " he began.

"Tell me."

"You're from Nainativu, aren't you?"

"Yes. Why?"

"No . . . I know an angel . . . sorry . . . a child called Raji from there . . . I need to meet her."

"She'll come to the festival. You'll be coming tomorrow, won't you?"

"Why tomorrow? I'll come this very evening."

"We can meet her there."

James stood up.

"Forgive me for calling you here. If I hadn't had this stomach problem, I would have come to your rooms. Thank you so much for coming," James said.

"That's alright. It was no trouble at all," Thiravi replied.

9

"RAJIII . . . !" THIYAGU HOWLED AS he rushed in suddenly that morning, and Raji was immediately frightened. Kamala was startled too, and wondered what was going on. It took her a while to calm him down and ask what was going on.

Thiyagu wept as if he had lost his very foundation. It was understandable. He had no place to go when he left the camp. He had to struggle to buy himself even a cup of tea. It was Veerabaku who had taken him in, without even knowing who or what he was. It was that foundation he had lost.

Veerabaku had given him a cup of tea that he had been holding, clutched his chest, and then Veerabaku slid down to the floor. Hearing his cries of "Aiyo," the neighbouring shopkeeper came by, looked at Veerabaku and said, "It's all over, there's no use taking him to a hospital either."

Vithuran, who had been standing beside him, understood that he too had lost something and began to cry. Raji called him and hugged him. He was a child of the island. No matter where he was born, he was of Nesamalar's blood. She had searched for a life for herself all over the place, and though the way she had died was nothing to be proud of, that drive . . . that search . . . it was all a tradition of the island.

Raji and Kamala had been getting ready to attend the festival. At first, they felt annoyed and frustrated that Thiyagu had come in search of them. Veerabaku had never gone to the Ceylonese folks' houses nearby or got to know them. He only stayed to talk to a couple of the men on the street. So, it was unavoidable that he would remain an anonymous corpse, unclaimed.

Raji knew that the trouble wouldn't end with his funeral either. Even if she didn't consider Thiyagu a problem, Vithuran was certainly a problem. Yet no one could leave a Lankan man's body unclaimed like this. How could another Lankan do it?

"Kamala akka, what shall we do?" Raji asked.

Her question implied that something had to be done. She couldn't herself decide what they could do. But Raji was used to dealing with these kinds of crises in some form or another. And since she had some savings from her job at a nearby public call office, she didn't need to hesitate too much to take on the task.

"We need to do something, don't we?" Kamala replied.

That was enough. She took Kamala and Thiyagu with her and went to Veerabaku's house. "Poor man, he was a gentle soul," the shopkeeper neighbour, who had stayed behind, said sympathetically as he left.

Outside, the vehicles flew by carrying goods and people. People sped by on bicycles.

Life needs such movement.

Life also needs mercy.

There is a need for a few anonymous people to take over the funeral rites for a third anonymous person.

"Wait a moment, akka. I'll come back," Raji said as she rushed out to the street "Santhan annai!" she called out and clapped her hands. Santhan turned his cycle around and came up to her. Raji explained the situation to him.

"My sister and family have come from Norway . . . mm . . . what to do? . . . this is important too," he murmured, almost to himself. "We're the Ceylonese folks here. We must take care of it! Wait a while. I'll go find a car and send them off and come. They're planning to go out somewhere."

"Okay. You go and come."

When Santhan came back a short while later, the arrangements were quickly made to have the body removed.

Santhan got the medical certificate to confirm the death was due to natural causes, delivered it to the police station and paid for the permission to have the body buried out of his own pocket. It was all done by twelve o'clock. The cemetery was not far either. Veerabaku's funeral procession began at one o'clock. After the burial was done, everyone returned home by two.

The landlord gave them an account for around three hundred rupees in costs. "I have the five thousand rupees advance he gave me on the rent. After deducting a thousand for this month's rent, I can give you the remaining four thousand when you move his things out. I can deduct the three hundred from that as well," he said. "And . . . he has a debit of around two hundred and change at the shop," he didn't forget to add.

Kumarasamy's house sent them some lunch. Kumarasamy had also said that Thiyagu and Vithuran could come and spend the night at their house for the next couple of days if they needed to. For the moment, the problem was solved.

Kamala and Raji bathed, got dressed again, and went to the festival.

When they got there, Raji felt they should have stayed at home. She wondered for a long while why they had bothered to rush there and could think of no reason. It was difficult to believe that a lot of people she knew would be there.

When they gave out the tea, her uncertainty and lethargy vanished. Before the tea arrived at her section, Thiravi called her. "Come over here. I need to speak to you in private. Come, let's go out somewhere and drink some coffee."

She went with him.

They met Viswalingam along the way. He had come to attend the festival too. He asked them how they were. "I went to Assam . . . somehow found where your sister-in-law lives. She's coming here next week. Your mother . . . she's so excited, she can't contain herself."

She assured him that she would visit his family and spend some time there and walked on.

Her mother's calm face danced before her eyes. When amma was happy, she looked like a goddess. When she thought of amma's joy, it was as if her heart was tickled with a peacock feather. A fountain of serenity had begun flowing in her own heart already.

She had thought that Thiravi too might try to compel her to go back to Suthan. But she wasn't afraid of that today. Because amma was beginning to value individual feelings and reasoning over obsessing about what people around her thought of them. It was no small thing that she had sent Viswalingam to bring the mother and child, with no care for what people would say. Raji still didn't know what she was going to do. But she knew, at the very least, that her mother would ensure they had some social status and the means to live.

As they walked, Thiravi broke the silence between them. He told her that she had grown. She thought he probably meant that she had grown older and laughed to herself.

There were grey strands in his hair too. But he hadn't shrunk.

They sat across from each other at the shop and ordered coffee. He allowed the conversation to drift to small talk before turning it to his own concerns. "How is your relationship with Arasi? Just the same as before? Or . . . ?"

"It's the same as before. Why?"

"A person can only discuss their personal matters with someone they're really close to, no?"

She looked at him in surprise. When had he ever spoken so tenderly in his life?

He laughed. Lightly. It seemed to beg her to reply.

"Arasi and I are just the same as we were before. But Arasi hasn't mentioned anything personal to me!" she replied.

He was silent for a while and then sighed deeply.

Was he blowing away the castles he had built in the air? She was stunned.

He spoke almost to himself: "Maybe . . . there's nothing personal in her heart to share?"

She thought she understood now what he meant.

He picked up his coffee.

He gestured for her to drink hers too.

"There isn't anything definite yet. But I feel something in my heart. The beginnings of it. I still need to figure it out. Maybe . . . if the other person is clear . . . it would be easier for me to identify what it is too," he said softly.

She could see that he was hesitant to reveal his feelings. Had it been twenty years ago, there would have been no hesitation in coming out with it. At that age, loving and losing was only painful. In his forties, it would be an embarrassment. That's what Thiravi was afraid of.

He laughed. He had come back to himself now. "At this age, no great needs come up. You can put your mind to important things and forget those needs altogether and get on with your life. The heart is like a fruit. It must ripen on its own on the branch and fall as it falls, with no desire of winning or losing. Becoming attached to another person . . . creates some complications for someone with the family situation I have. If it is a loving relationship, then those problems don't feel heavy. If not . . . at some point . . . I might come to regret it," he said.

She felt as if he was including her in what he said.

She felt he had a greater determination in his step on their way back to the auditorium than when they had left. He was the old Thiravi again. The one who had set aside a life of desires.

10

ARASI REMEMBERED THE CONVERSATION she had had with her mother the previous night.

"Will the festival end on Sunday, Arasi?"

"Yes, amma."

"When it ends, everyone who came here for the festival will go back. No . . . ?"

"Yes, why?"

"Will maami also go back?"

"She didn't come for the festival. But she might make arrangements to go back after the festival is over."

"The matter we came for is finished. What are we going to do here. Why don't we leave?"

Seeing her mother sunk in thought wherever they went, Arasi could somewhat guess the direction of her thoughts. As she was undecided on the issue herself, she hadn't paid much attention to it.

She said, "I thought about that too. It's going to cost a lot of money for two people to travel now. That's why I put the thought aside."

"Even if we stay here, we're not earning to feed ourselves, are we?"

Did she mean that they should ask someone's help?

"We have to, don't we?" Valambikai said.

She could see that amma had decided to go back home. She felt a slight unease that she had been so distracted that she hadn't been thinking about it herself.

She was resolved that they wouldn't expect any more help from Maheswari.

Valambikai's question hovered between them unanswered.

They had bought some bread and made tea for their dinner. Things were okay for them. But that day she had terrible indigestion. Until she fell asleep, and even while she slept, she suffered from heartburn.

Whenever she saw Suthan at the festival she felt as if a part of her own body had grown away from her and was walking about. She could have gone up to him and asked him about his recovery from the bullet wound. Amma had gone up to him on the first day and talked to him. She had asked him to come by the house for a meal. Suthan had hesitated, saying he wondered what akka would say. Amma had told her all about it. She told her he had cried; she had cried talking about it. It could be true. That's how his face looked at that moment. She had seen it. He had kept turning to look at her as though he was calling out for her: akka . . . akka.

What was the barrier between them? Their values had changed. It wasn't just him; she too had left their homeland. She would return. He wouldn't. There was no great difference in that, was there? They just needed something to break through their uncertainty and open a way for them to speak to each other.

She fell asleep with that thought.

As she travelled from Ayanavaram to Porur the next day, Arasi thought back on all this.

It was nine by the time she reached home. After she ate, she and Raji brought chairs out to the front yard and chatted. Kamala stayed inside, saying that the mist would get in and it wouldn't agree with her.

The sky . . . the clouds . . . the stars . . . there was beauty in the night.

The breeze was comforting.

They spoke for a long time. Then Raji said, "All the drama will be over tomorrow."

"Mm."

"What are you planning to do?"

"I am hoping to go back. Amma will come with me. I don't know where to get the money for the tickets."

"Why, can't you ask Suthan?"

Her answer was hesitant. "We need to ask him. But I'm just not sure how . . . "

"If you tell amma, she'll ask him, no problem."

"That's what we'll have to do."

Was she never going to speak to Suthan again? Raji wanted to ask her. But what would she do if Arasi turned the same question around on her?

Raji felt angry that they now had to rethink what they stood for in the light of the present situation. There were many forms in which they could pursue their freedom. An armed rebellion was one form. It was the form she aligned with. Thiravi was opposed to it. He was a conscientious objector. Arasi evaluated the reasoning behind the functions and activities of the struggle. When there was such a range of positions, how could she justify her anger at Suthan anymore?

Just last month the Elephant Pass base had fallen. It had been an impregnable military base up to then. Yogesh had a role in that victory. Even if it was just a small one.

Her relationship with him was inexplicable. Yet it could be explained if she only thought about it. She had simply not wished to understand it thus far. She still bore the scars. The pain remained inside. Did it matter if the wound had healed a thousand days ago? Or ten thousand? It still hurt occasionally.

She wanted a blanket. Not for the cold, but to hide in. To hide from everyone. She felt the cold too. But it wasn't the reason she wished for a blanket.

She was fixed on what Arasi had told her the previous day. She believed it. She believed it because it was him. Then she second-guessed herself. When she thought more about it, she had decided it couldn't be him. Because she strongly believed that if he came to Chennai he would be at her house within the hour. She knew the extent of his devotion to her.

She felt that Arasi hadn't mentioned it to anyone else because she wasn't entirely sure herself.

They were both absorbed in their own thoughts when Kamala brought them back to reality:

"Of all the people we know who left the island, very few are doing well."

She had been sunk in her own thoughts too.

Many of the people they knew were not doing well at all. Suthan, Rajendran, Raji, Nesamalar . . .

Then, as she remembered Nesamalar's child, Kamala went on, "I feel sorry for Vithuran. His foster father is dead now. He's left with someone who doesn't even know how to take care of himself. Who knows what will happen to that child tomorrow? How will he end up?"

They went to bed.

Outside, the heavy vehicles roared intermittently as they flew by. It sounded like the growl of demons as they passed.

11

Chennai, India

WHEN EVENTS HAPPEN IN some order, it feels as though time rolls by easily. There is some joy to be found in everyday tasks. When tragedies strike, we panic, and life becomes disordered and slow. Order is part of the equation. Speed and slowness can become predictable.

The three of them had woken up early that day. Arasi had bathed, and now it was Raji's turn. In the kitchen, Kamala was busy preparing their breakfast.

"Okay, I'm getting ready now, Raji. Why don't you come along, we can visit Thiyagu," Arasi said as she got ready to leave.

"How are you going? It will take a long time if you go by bus. Take an auto," Kamala said.

"That will be too expensive."

"You have to go if it's important. There's an auto driver nearby, whom we know well. Take that one. We can give him the money later."

Kumarasamy's house was just a little past the bus stop.

When they got to Thiyagu's, he was sitting with his head in his hands, thinking. Raji was surprised to see that he didn't react when he saw her. She was everything to him because Suthan

wasn't around. But he was sunk in a profound grief, both oblivi-
ous and motionless.

"Thiyagu!" Raji called.

"Mm."

"Look, can you tell me who's come to see you?"

He turned around and looked at Arasi.

His gaze rose to her face and slid away; he shook his head, no.

"Look closer. She's from our island . . . "

When Raji prompted him again, he sat up. He stared at her for
a while. He squinted at her the way he used to back home in the
village. His face brightened a little. "You . . . you . . . you're Suthan's
akka, aren't you? You still have the scar from the mango sap near
your mouth," he said.

His khaki trousers had gone. He was wearing a sarong. He had
grown slim. He wasn't gaunt, he had just lost some of his plumpness.

Arasi thought he seemed a little clearer in his mind, too.

He was thinking . . . identifying people . . . he wasn't rambling
or asking endless questions . . . wasn't all this a sign that he was
getting stronger, mentally?

Raji was thrilled. Even his sadness was a sign of his clarity.

Raji asked him, "What are you thinking so hard about,
Thiyagu?"

"Tch. Nothing."

"Just tell me."

"Veerabaku died so suddenly, didn't he? That's what I was
thinking about."

"Why, because the child he was raising is now your
responsibility?"

"Whether anyone says it or not, Vithu is my responsibility now,
isn't he?"

He didn't have a means to feed himself. What would he do with
a child? Raji wondered but said nothing.

"He said he was going to take me with him when he went back to the village."

"To the village? When?"

"Soon."

"He was going to get you a ticket and take you with him? He was truly a good man."

"After two days of getting to know each other, he took to me, but we weren't going to take a ticket and go on a plane . . . we were going by boat."

"In a boat?"

"Mm. Someone came here two days ago. He came here in a boat. He said he would take us with him when he went back."

"Who was that? Do you know the man?" Arasi asked quickly.

He thought for a while and said no.

"And if you go to the village . . . Sinthamani . . . ?" Raji asked.

"Sinthamani won't come again. She must have died somewhere, like Veerabaku."

Was this the first time he had fully grasped death?

"Very well. Your friend Suthan has come from abroad—didn't you see him?"

He turned to look at her, unmoved.

Then he shook his head, as of to say no to himself: "What's there to see? I came here eager to see Suthan. I waited for so long. Suthan didn't come to see me, did he?"

"Maybe Suthan doesn't know."

"Mm. You don't talk to him anymore. Who else will tell him that I'm here? Maybe you're right. I'll try to see him if I can, before I go."

"Are you going to the village by yourself?"

"With Vithu."

Raji was amazed that he planned to take Vithu with him.

Just then a child came up to the entrance, "Thiyagu . . . " he whined. It was Vithuran.

"That colouring . . . those eyes . . . poor thing . . . how she had strayed and been ruined, finally. Now this child was an orphan. Though Thiyagu seems clearer in his mind now, he can't be a great help. And he too is a grown orphan," Raji thought.

Arasi tapped Raji, as if to say, "It's getting late, we must go." Raji understood. "Okay, Thiyagu. We'll leave now. We must go somewhere. We'll leave now, and I'll come back to see you," she said as she prepared to leave.

"Come to Veerabaku's house. I'll be going there in the afternoon."

"Why? What will you do on your own there? What will you do for food?"

"Kumarasamy's mother asked us to go there. We have to observe the eighth day. She said we can come there in the afternoon for four or five days and take some food with us."

"Then?"

"Then we'll go back to the village."

"Don't rush into anything. I'll come back in the evening, or tomorrow morning to see you. We'll think about what to do next later, okay?"

Thiyagu didn't say anything.

12

ONE DAY, SUTHAN WENT to the Air India ticket office to confirm his flight date, got on the bus at Anna Salai and went straight to Ayanavaram.

Arasi was at home. She saw him. She retreated into her shell, saying nothing. It was Valambikai who called him in. "Come, sit here."

He sat down. His eyers welled with tears. Valambikai burst into sobs. She ran inside and calmed herself and made some tea. She brought it out to him, and he sat there drinking it.

Eventually they recovered from the waves of emotion that overtook them.

"I have to go back to France in a week, amma," he said quietly.

"We're going back to the village as well," Valambikai replied.

He looked at her as if to say, 'What do you hope to do there?'

"Whom do we have in this place, for us to stay here?" she said. She sounded slightly harsh. Then, as though she had just thought of something, "We didn't come here planning to stay either. It's better if we go back. I can take care of the farm garden with Arasi. We won't starve. How can we stay here and keep renting this place for seven hundred and fifty rupees every month?" she said.

He was silent.

The words kicked him gently.

He hesitated to say anything. He didn't want to say anything to stir up old memories and start another fight. But he couldn't bear it. "The fighting isn't over there."

"When will that end? Nobody believes it will ever end. Death will come somehow. It's a blessing if we die there," Valambikai retorted. "But for us to go . . . you need to give us the money. For both of us."

Arasi turned to look. Why did she look? She turned away again quickly.

He paused, as if he was calculating something in his mind. Then he said: "I can do that. After I pay off my room when I'm leaving, I'll have about fifteen thousand left. I'll give you that. I'll have to send the remainder when I get to France."

"Send money for our expenses too."

"Mm."

Later, as though she just thought of it, she said, "Have you given up entirely on Raji?"

"What can I do now? I have tried every way I can. Half my life is over. I must figure out a way to spend the rest of it. Nothing more I can do."

Arasi should have felt a little pity for him as he stood there, having lost all hope. She stopped in the middle of what she was doing and listened to him carefully.

He noticed it. How long it had been since his sister had hugged him! Wasn't his sibling's affection meant to be the shade on his half-complete journey towards old age? His eyes prickled.

"Don't cry. This is all the result of things you have done. Who else can do anything about it? Whom else can we blame for it?" his mother attempted to comfort him. "Oh God, why did these children end up like this?"

She had two children. Both their lives had ended up desolate. Then she said, "I . . . if you want, I can have Arasi ask her about it?"

He laughed.

Was he so despairing? His last source of hope for straightening out his life was vanishing from him. Arasi saw it and was taken aback.

"Why?" Valambikai asked.

"What's left to ask, amma? If it's meant to be, it will happen on its own."

"You were more than halfway meant to be. What happened to it? Maami isn't saying anything. Wait and see, at the last minute she'll find a way somehow to send her along with you."

After a few moments of silence, "When will you bring the money?" she asked.

"The day before I leave. I'll bring it myself."

He stood up. "The sun has climbed. Winter sun. I have some work to do. I'll see you, amma."

"Okay. Have you gone to see Maheswari maami?"

"No."

"Go see her once. Rajendran's woman and child are there. You'll get to see them as well."

"I'll go tomorrow."

He came and stood in front of Arasi for a while.

Seeing him there, her heart pleaded, "Look up . . . look up . . . " Arasi looked up.

He stumbled slightly and said, "I'll see you akka," and turned around and walked away briskly.

13

Chennai, India

SUTHAN WALKED AROUND FOR a long while before he
went back to his room. By the time he washed, went down for his
dinner, and went to bed, it was ten o'clock.

It was as if all the rain had evaporated, and the earth was boil-
ing again. He had walked all afternoon in the streets that were
heavy with glare, heat, and dust, his own heart heavy.

He began to feel angry. He had thought over and over that the
small mistakes he had been thrust into by circumstance were for-
givable and felt angry that his belief had been overturned. This
was a species of anger. It was an anger that took hold when the
body was at the mercy of its needs. Human nature is as much
composed of vices as it is of virtues.

The evening dew was done now. It was the season when dew
came later at night. Solitude was a torment at times when the
body was taken over by need. Until the body bursts through the
dam of desires that haunt it and finds ease, the anger remains ele-
vated in the mind.

He lost his sleep to heat, desire, and memory, and lay in the dark.
He had decided he wouldn't chase after Raji anymore.

That was when his mother had asked, "Shall I try asking once, to see?" He rejected it. Not the person but the attempt. She must feel some need, desire, some longing too. If not, what was the use? This wasn't simply yoking one person to another. Neither was it a question of marrying for the sake of having children. It was simply the pull of life. That's why he had said it would happen if it was meant to,

She was no great beauty. But she had been as lush as the sculptures of Khajuraho. What else could he ask for in that four-and-a-half-foot body? She needed a willing heart. That was the most important.

He fell asleep while thinking. His eyelids closed and he felt his mind leap into the dark void of sleep. Just then a woman's lascivious laughter shattered his sleep. It could even be drunken laughter. He understood what that laughter meant at that time of day. He realized within a few moments that the sound emanated from the room directly above his and had floated out through the open window.

He couldn't go back to sleep after that. He didn't even try to. He waited for the thumping to begin upstairs. Ten . . . fifteen . . . twenty minutes later a vigorous thumping and the creaking of a bed floated down to him.

Desires can be contained. They allow themselves to be restrained too. It is the outside wind that stirs excitement within that calm. You must keep yourself away from the wind. After he and Sheila split, he had been fearful and huddled away from these winds. If you knew how to keep away from these enticing winds, you could easily be a hermit. He had proven it. But that day, suddenly on the wind . . . a tinge of excitement. He hurried to the light, switched it on and sat back down.

He could calm himself down. But it took a long time to fall asleep again.

It was busy at around nine the next morning. Awakened by the commotion, Suthan opened his red eyes and looked out the door.

People were going to and from the upper floor. Suthan realized the situation was serious only when a policeman came down the stairs. He asked the bell boy what had happened. "There has been a murder upstairs, in the room just above yours," he said, and Suthan froze in shock.

The inspector who came downstairs just then told the policemen accompanying him not to allow any of the hotel's occupants to leave, and to let them know he might have to question them.

Suthan closed the door, washed, and got dressed. Then he stepped outside his room to talk to the occupant in the opposite room. He had known him for two days. "It's one of your people, sir. He had a Ceylonese passport in his bag. Who knows when the murderer came, but he killed him without a noise and left. He put a bullet through his ear, sir. Why sir, who could kill a man by putting a bullet through his ear?"

Suthan came back inside and sat thinking.

He wondered if any of the neighbouring folks had mentioned the "good time" that had happened the night before.

Someone knocked on his door.

He opened it.

"Are you Sri Lankan?" a man who looked like he might be the sub-inspector asked him.

"Yes. But I live in France now."

"Let's see, take out your passport."

He took it out and showed it to him.

It was a French government-issued passport. His entry stamp and Indian visa were all in order. He had been staying in the hotel for ten days now. The murdered man had been there only for three. There was no reason to suspect him. The sub-inspector let him go.

When he went downstairs, he questioned the manager. "The man gave his address as Meesalai in Jaffna, sir. He brought a woman here last night saying it was his relative and had a good time. Your people. Some of them behave very badly, sir," he said.

"What was the man's name?"

"Kanthasamy Nadaraja."

14

Chennai, India

THIYAGU HAD GONE BACK to Veerabaku's place, as he had said. He took care of the child himself. The landlord lent them anything essential they needed. He now got his food from Kamala's in the afternoons.

Kamala spoke to Raji that afternoon. "I'm thinking of asking Thiyagu and the child to come and stay here, Raji. What do you think? He can tell the landlord that he's letting go of the house this month as well."

"It's incredible how Thiyagu seems to be able to think and act so clearly, after he took responsibility for the child. His haziness isn't there anymore. I think we can ask him to stay here without worrying about anything, Kamala akka," Raji replied.

"When he comes for lunch, we can let him know and tell him to gradually bring his things over and keep them here."

It was getting to be three in the afternoon. As she finished the movie she was watching on the television, Kamala said, "Raji, it's so late and there's no sign of Thiyagu? Be a good child and go run and see what's happening, will you? Maybe he's asleep or something?"

"He'll come akka . . . let's wait a while and see," Raji said in a tired voice.

"Go, Raji. Poor Vithu."

Raji didn't argue anymore. She got up and left. Veerabaku's house was not far from Kamala's. There were two shops and about eight houses in between. Seeing Raji walking by at a quick pace, the landlord tried to call out to her. But she had opened the gate and gone in by then. Seeing a padlock dangling from the door, she froze with surprise.

Where was Thiyagu? Where was Vithu? A suspicion began to stir in her mind. She went back to the landlord.

"I don't see anyone at the house?"

"Yes, I only noticed it this afternoon, myself. Then I remembered that I hadn't seen them since the morning. I waited for a long time; they didn't come. The door was open as well. Yes, so I thought I'll wait for a while and come and ask you about it."

"The lock?"

"I put it on there, wondering if it was a good idea to leave the place open like that."

She turned back.

She gave Kamala the report on her return.

"He said he had booked something with a boatman. If the man came, he was going to go with him . . . poor fool, it looks like he's gone back to the village with the child," Kamala said in shock.

"That's what I think too, akka."

"What do we do now?"

"What can we do? It's God's plan."

"He didn't breathe a word to us."

"He must have thought if he told us we'd say something to stop him, akka. That's why he has done this."

The afternoon was unexciting.

Arasi came by at five. That was unusual. It was the first time she had come there unannounced.

Arasi felt that Suthan had come by that morning only to disrupt her peace. Even though she had kept silent and turned away from him, he had come to say goodbye to her before he left. It wasn't just his words, but his tone, and his pitiable state that broke through the barriers of her rejection.

When she turned, he was gone. Had he stayed a little longer, she might have shaken her head. Had the opportunity escaped them because of her hesitation or his haste?

She had cried. A final moment of heartbreak. But she survived it. That was when she knew she would always retain some small feeling of compassion for him.

She didn't know what to do with herself.

She thought she would go see Raji. She could try talking to her. But it was her decision in the end. No one had the right to deny her that. She may have retreated into herself and kept herself shielded, like Arasi had. Her mother still hoped for an answer from her. She might try to convince her just one more time before she left for Canada. Even if she refused, they could at least ask her for her reasons. She thought they may not be anything obvious to others.

"Suthan came home this morning," Arasi said to Raji. "Amma asked him for money. He says he'll give it to her. He has to go back and send it from there."

Raji realized that Arasi had not brought Suthan up in conversation before. Still, her attachment to him must still be strong.

They walked up to the balcony together. Arasi sat on the ledge and said: "Suthan will go to France in a week. Who knows when we'll see these people after they leave? That must have been on his mind when he tried to speak to me for the very first time today. I didn't speak to him. But I will, before he goes."

Raji said nothing.

Arasi broke the silence that had fallen between them to ask: "And you?" She didn't have the heart to say any more.

"What about me?"

"Do you want to talk to him someday?"

"About what?"

"About anything."

"If I ever must . . . then . . . I will."

"You're angry with him because he lived with Sheila."

"That's nothing to me. I swear. But how can I tell you the reason?"

Arasi's doubts grew as she kept refusing to talk about it.

They talked about several other things, like Thiraviyam leaving and Maheswari's trip. But she completely and obstinately refused to even touch on the topic that had begun their conversation.

They heard Kamala call out. "Come down, both of you. Someone's here for you."

"Who? Could it be Thiyagu?" Raji rushed downstairs in a whirl.

Thiravi stood there. "I went to Arasi's place. Her mother said she had come here. So I thought I may as well come and see you too," he said.

They went in.

"What is it?" Arasi asked.

"There was a murder in Suthan's hotel last night. A Sri Lankan, they say."

"Is he in any trouble?"

"Nothing like that. But the dead man's name sounded familiar. I remember that you had mentioned it to me, and I put two and tow together, and got an answer to a question that was puzzling me. I wanted to tell you right away, so I rushed over."

"Who was the dead man?"

"Someone from Meesalai."

"Name?"

"Kanthasamy Nadaraja."

"I don't know who that could be . . . "

"You don't know? Squint-eyed Nadaraja. Do you remember that name?"

Arasi froze. The "scarecrow" who had been responsible for Rakini's death, squint-eyed Nadaraja.

She thought of Rakini. The girl who had fueled her poetic impulse. Her own poetry didn't have half the reach of Rakini's. She calmed herself to say, "Did you know the man personally?"

"No, I didn't."

"Did you see the body yourself?"

"No."

"Then how can you say he was squint-eyed Nadaraja?"

"Wasn't he from Meesalai?"

"There must be a hundred Nadarajas in Meesalai. There must be at least ten Kanthasamy Nadarajas."

"True. But if you work it out, this is the answer," he said and laughed. "This is a method of deducing events through probabilities. You can predict events this way too."

"Tell me in a way that I can understand."

"Look here. There was a Meesalai Nadaraja murdered in the hotel. Around ten days ago you said you had seen two boys from the Iyakkam who looked like Yogesh and someone else. You said at the time you thought it was possible they had come here to do something wrong. You were afraid that they might have come here to take down someone who had come for the Assembly festival. But they had really come to take down Squint-eyed Nadaraja."

"Arasi said she had seen two men who looked like Yogesh and Puvanendi. How can you say for certain that it was Yogesh and Puvanendi?" Raji asked.

"Because the murdered man is squint-eyed Nadaraja."

His logic seemed to make sense.

Arasi and Thiravi walked together to the bus.

15

Chennai, India

MAHESWARI SAT UNMOVING ON the verandah, her eyes directed to the other side of the street, as far as she could; she couldn't bear to look at anyone. Senan sat across from her in the same pose. Saraswathi sat a little beyond them. Thulasi and the other children beside her. Amba and her child sat to a side. Mala was inside.

What had happened in this house?

Senan, who had not come home for a few days and returned that day. At the door he had yelled, "Hey you, Mala!"

When Mala came out, he grabbed her like a like a little chicken. "I'm going to kill you right now!" he roared. He held her by the throat against the wall with one hand, while the other swung out as if he was about to slap her as hard as he could.

Just then Maheswari, who had gone out with Amba and the child, returned, and got out of the auto at the entrance. Seeing him, she cried out, "Senaaa . . . !" and ran in.

Senan's grip loosened and he dropped his hand.

"What kind of work is this? To do this to a woman? Come here . . . don't you know how to act like a human being?"

She had lost her composure. She now lived in a country where there were laws against mistreating not only women and children, but also dogs, cats, birds, rabbits, and other domesticated animals. She had internalized some of that ahimsa. She was furious.

Senan, who had moved away from Mala now, burst out, "Aren't I her own thambi? But I have to stay here twiddling my thumbs. Her husband's brother has to go abroad and earn. Sheila akka and maami sent her husband abroad. Now he sends money from there . . . this one stays here and bosses us around. Shouldn't she have sent me abroad first, maami, when I'm right in front of her eyes?"

"What is this, Mala? What is Senan talking about?"

Hearing the family's troubles distressed her too.

"Who am I to look out for, maami? Should I take care of my brother? Or his brother? I must do as he says, no?"

"You can't do as he says here," Saraswathi butted in. "If he went abroad on his own money he can do as he likes. He went abroad with our child's help, our people's help; he must take care of us first, no? Isn't that so, Maheswari akka; what do you say?"

"Don't drag me into these kinds of family disputes, Saraswathi," Maheswari tried to wriggle out of it.

Saraswathi was having none of it. "You can't say that akka. What's right is right anywhere, isn't it? Why do we need to see someone's face to hear what they have to say? Look here now. It's three months since Sheila sent us any money. If it goes on like this, should I take these children and go jump in front of a train somewhere? If Senan goes, he can earn and get these girls married off, can't he?"

"There's a girl in his family too. She's his older sister. Isn't it important that the older one gets settled first?" Mala countered.

"You didn't think about the girls right here. But the girl over there came to your eye. Is that so?"

"These ones have time."

"That's a good one." Saraswathi wiggled her body in mockery. Amba felt herself about to burst into laughter. She contained it and stood staring at them. Saraswathi went on: "Senan has been waiting for five years. The day he started talking about going abroad, he stopped going to school. Here they talk about English school . . . Tamil school . . . I don't understand anything about the schools here. I don't even know what Senan has studied. Now it looks like he has learned to read and write a little. That's all the education he has. What job can he get here with that? She didn't think about any of this . . . this . . . this one keeps talking about that one's brother."

Maheswari understood the situation now. She understood what had damaged the relationship between Saraswathi and Mala. Though she had offered her own help for Mala's sake, shouldn't the benefits that came from it go to her family? Shouldn't they at least experience the first fruits of that effort? She explained this gently.

"What you say is true, maami. But there . . . he has to think about his family's situation too, doesn't he? His parents have said 'Do whatever you want after you take Param abroad . . . '"

"You should think about your own brother first, shouldn't you, child?"

"I never said that I wouldn't send him."

"When? In another two or three years . . . after we have paid off all this debt?" Senan growled.

"How do we know what he'll want in another two or three years? I kept beating my head over it, that we should send Senan first. Okay, she didn't need to send anyone else, she could have gone herself, at least? If she had any sense, she would have. But this one wants to send her brother-in-law. What kind of child is this?" Saraswathi began crying. Then she came to herself, saying,

"All these years . . . she has been like a tree without a bud or a fruit. There isn't a day that has gone by that I haven't worried what that man will do, now that he's gone. And now, if he's sending for his brother . . . ?"

The fire of rage turned into a cloud of misery in her.

Crumpling under that revelation, Mala was unable to answer. She began trembling as though she was about to burst into tears and ran into her room.

She may have been crying because her mother had pointed out that she was barren. But it was Saraswathi's suspicion that her husband's love was fake that broke her heart.

You couldn't blame her for saying it. She suspected it because it was possible. In a way, suspicions arise from possibilities, don't they?

Maheswari sat there for a long time.

How was that a tiny little island woman was able to weigh every movement and atom so accurately? This was the question that unfurled in her mind as she began to emerge from the misery of the situation. Her surprise didn't leave her even as she came back to reality. She stood and walked up to Senan. "Don't worry about anything, Sena. I'll tell Mala to send Param later."

"Param is surely in London by now, maami. It's because she did everything behind our backs . . . that's why I lost my temper when I found out. Wouldn't anyone feel the same, maami?"

Maheswari understood his explosion now. There was nothing more to do. All she could do was to pacify Senan. "Never mind, let it go," she said. "I will tell Mala that she must send you next. If something comes up and she doesn't send you within the next two years, I will do it myself, okay? Be a good boy, stay out of trouble. Amba will be here for a while. Praba will be going to school here. You have to be here and give her all the help she needs. I must go to Canada and talk to Viji and decide what we can do about

Amba. Amba said she needs to go back to her village once. Appa will go with her. If you can, you go too. Don't breathe a word to anyone about me sending you abroad. Let's see if Mala does it. If not, I'm here, okay?"

"Okay, maami."

"I'll be leaving for Canada on the fifteenth. Don't roam around with these trouble-making boys. I'll call once in a while and check up on you. Understood?"

Senan nodded his head and went inside and sat down.

They turned on the lights.

Maheswari coughed lightly.

The dew was a little heavy that day.

16

Chennai, India

KAMALA HAD LEFT EARLY that morning for Mangadu to offer her prayers or fulfill a vow. The Mangadu Amman was her regular deity. She had made offerings, vows and prayers to her. Amman had responded by blessing her. Her requests were very reasonable. She prayed that the arthritis in her arms and legs wouldn't give her trouble during the cold season; her husband should find a good job; and that he should somehow come for a visit the next year at least. She would pray for the well-being of others as well, during her general prayers, and that was all. She didn't take on any vows for anyone else because her body couldn't fulfill them. It kept getting bloated. Perhaps she was fulfilling her vow because Nagaraja had written saying he was coming for the April New Year, or because she hadn't been in as much pain through the rainy, foggy weather. If Kamala went to Mangadu, she would stay for a whole afternoon, eat the rice blessed by the goddess, and watch all the rituals before she returned. She had left at around seven in the morning but wouldn't be back before seven or eight that night.

It was nine when Kamala returned home. She had a basket and a rolled-up evening newspaper in her hands. Her face was downcast . . . tired . . . like a sky overcome with clouds.

"Kamala akka, why, didn't you get a bus?" Raji who had been reading on the verandah asked in concern. "What is it, Kamala akka? Why are you looking so upset?"

It was only as she stood up that she noticed that not only was her face darkened, but that she had been crying. Wet streaks on her face, tears in her eyes. She looked as though she had stopped at the gate and cried before entering.

"Akka . . . !" Raji said kindly as she brought her in, took the bag from her hands, leaned her against the wall and held her hand. "Wait here. I'll make you some tea and be right back."

Kamala watched her without moving. Was there something in her eyes that looked like sympathy for Raji?

"What is it, akka?"

Before she could finish her sentence, Kamala stretched out the newspaper.

"What is it? Oh . . . does she want me to read the paper?" Raji wondered. She took it and opened it out. She looked at the headlines. Politics. Second headline . . . political parties. Third headline . . . nothing. A small text box below:

The Sri Lankan Navy shot down a boat belonging to the Tigers as it attempted to enter their territorial waters and sank it. It is believed the boat may have been carrying medical supplies. The navy was able to identify four Tigers using night binoculars. They were only able to retrieve one body and believe the other three rebels may have escaped. An official from the Sri Lankan navy described it as a great success in their intensive patrolling of the area. The body retrieved belonged to a boat navigator identified as Yogesh, who had caused great losses to the Sri Lankan navy, and had proven to be a challenge to them, he further announced.

'Yogesh!' her soul called out. And she crumbled within.

She had sent him to become a rebel. He had eased her disappointments in life by becoming a rebel. She had not given him any great pleasure. If she was honest, it had never been pleasure. It had been a trap.

For the intimacy of one day, he had done his duty for fifteen years in the homeland, and finally given his life to it. He had desired that union out of love for her. But she, no matter how stirred she had been by the sensuous sculptures, she had not lain with him out of love. It had been a trap. She had made herself a trap. Through an exchange.

"Oh God!" she cried out. She pressed her hand to her chest. Not knowing her true distress, Kamala said, "That's how I felt as soon as I saw the news, too."

"Akka . . . ah . . . !" Unable to hold back the height of her sobs, Raji ran into her room.

If crying was the only way to ease her sorrow, let her cry. Kamala did not follow her. She went to the hearth and peered into the rice pot. There was a little rice. Raji could have it. She had no appetite. Kamala went in and lay down.

He had stayed in her house for a few days. Fifteen years ago, now. He had seemed bent on victory, and determined, but he also had humility. It made it easy for anyone to love him. It was natural for her to feel sad at his death. But it didn't exceed the limits of a natural grief. Thiyagu and Vithu could have been with him, she had thought. But she couldn't be certain. She couldn't grieve for them yet.

Kamala fell asleep shortly after.

When she woke up to use the washroom, Kamala looked in on Raji. The door to her room was still ajar, as it had been when Kamala had gone to bed. Though there was no light from inside, she felt sure that Raji was still awake and went closer to look. Raji was seated on her bed, staring out into the darkness through the window. She looked as though she was wiping her face over and over with her hand. Was Raji still crying? Was it her grief about this loss, was it because there was so much one after another to grieve about, or was it because she was grieving thinking about Thiyagu and Vithu? Why . . . why . . . why?

When she went back to lie down, sleep didn't come as easily as it had the first time. Her mind replayed the past, bumping into closed doors and fortresses in search of the reason for Raji being as crushed as she was. She had wondered about this a few years ago, could it be?

She thought it over.

Raji had been in the Keelputhupet refugee camp. That was the time when she had turned her attention furiously towards the wellbeing of the refugees. She would come up from Keelputhupet once a month to visit the Organization for Eelam Refugee Rehabilitation. She used to like to stay with Kamala in Anna Nagar when she had to stay in town for a day or two. No matter how she seemed in the camp, when she came to Kamala's she seemed like someone who had lost everything, barely holding on to herself. It was at that time that Yogesh had appeared. Raji, who had been sunk in thought, like a wandering spirit, had become clear in a minute. "Will you come with me, Yogesh? Let's go to Mahabalipuram," she had said to him. Kamala had been stunned by the way she had asked it. She was well-read herself. She didn't only read the news; she enjoyed the social and political mass journals as well. It wasn't for the sake of understanding the social political condition of the outside world. It was her eagerness for the information they provided. It was the sort of thing the masses had a taste for. Their specialness was in gathering information more and more to taste and spit it out!

The day after Raji returned from her trip with Yogesh, she had sat in her room crying for a long time. At the time, Kamala had a mild suspicion that Raji's tears were at the loss of something deeper. She had thought at the time that the way men and women behaved with each other had changed in nature, in their society. When she had left her country, things hadn't been that way either there or here. Now it was. Nowadays, she was hearing a lot about women who lifted a self-loading rifle to their shoulders, finding their targets as effortlessly as men did. They had been turning their weaknesses into strengths. A failed romantic relationship or failed marriage didn't affect them the same way anymore. These were the signs of a new world being born. Even though they were not the only signs. It was her knowledge that had made her suspicious then.

What despair she must have felt to run to her room crying, "Yogesh . . . !" She had lost him. If that was true, wasn't it also true that she had possessed him?

She went from confusion to clarity, and back into confusion again. She went to make a cup of tea to calm herself. Then she sat for a while in the hall, drinking it.

Raji's door was closed now. When had she fallen asleep? When Kamala went to it slowly and touched it with her fingers, the door swung open slightly. Kamala looked in. Raji was standing at the window.

Kamala slowly began to understand it all clearly now. She didn't want to be a bother.

Two days passed.

Kamala came out to the front yard because she didn't see Raji in the house. When she looked up, she saw Raji seated on the low wall of the balcony with her back to her, looking out to the west.

Kamala went upstairs.

Raji's gaze was fixed on the red sun sinking into the western horizon. Though her gaze was fixed, it seemed that none of the images made an impression on her eyes. There were no signs that she had cried, or was crying, either.

Raji came to and turned when she called her for the second time. "What?" she asked, as though she had only paused her thoughts for the moment.

Kamala didn't reply but went and sat beside her.

The balcony had not been swept, washed, or cleared for a while now. The young coconuts they had cut open for coconut water before the monsoons sat drying, their mouths open in an O. The dried leaves shed by the jamun tree. The dust and husks.

She reminded her that they were like children of the same mother. She spoke of how the relationship had grown between them over thirteen or fourteen years. She had been this close to her because she had never thought they had one face inside and shown another outside.

"What about it, akka? Why are you bringing this up now?" Raji said blankly.

"Because . . . you have only shown me a half of yourself in all these years that you've known me. I never expected that."

"What are you talking about akka?"

"I'm talking about what's obvious to me. Don't lie to me. Answer my question now. I'm sad about Yogesh's death too. Why are you so heartbroken?"

Raji understood the direction Kamal was going in. How could she tell her that this wasn't half of herself? Not every event can be shared with everybody. There are some things that need to be kept between oneself and the person involved alone. Some things may need to stay hidden. How was it a crime to conceal what was meant to be concealed?

She wasn't sure what to do anymore. As far as there was no harm in Kamala knowing, there was no harm in her telling, she realized.

Raji moaned. "You met him and got to know him. He was a relative of mine. My mother's brother's son. He was my machan by birth."

"I know all that."

"But he was really more than that to me."

Kamala's gaze slid and settled onto her as if to say, 'Tell me in what way.'

"He was the man who fulfilled my desires."

Kamala was shaken. She hadn't expected such a blunt answer.

"I was registered in marriage to one man. He abandoned me and joined some random rebel faction. Though I didn't agree with his choice, I thought he had made the right decision and I accepted it. But the man didn't even stay in that group. He ran away abroad and lived in luxury. I left my country because of him. I left my amma and my thangachi. How many losses I bore for him. When I was falling apart thinking that there was no one to fight for the land I love, Yogesh said, 'I'm here, Raji,' and dedicated himself to the Movement. My soul tells me, in a way I'm responsible for his death. That's why this grief is more than I can bear," Raji said and stopped.

Kamala said nothing. There was nothing to say. She had thought one thing. But Raji seemed to embody a nationalist feeling more than anything else.

The fading light helped them return to themselves. Two beings, motionless beneath an expanse of sky. Their souls worn away by conscience, they wept in silence.

Raji spoke: "Isn't it a betrayal to send someone else to fight on your behalf, akka? Now, I must suffer the loss of him and bear the crime of causing his death."

Raji stepped down from the ledge. She peered at the sky overhead. Was Yogesh there?

As her confusion cleared, she straightened. "It's not right for me to escape any more."

As though understanding her mind, Kamala said, "Not every-one can do battle. Not everyone has the maturity and physical strength to go to war. That's not a great crime. Now look, you know some people yourself, you told me there are still some of them in the camp, some people who get up in the middle of the night and run around screaming 'The heli* is coming, the heli is coming.' What's their sickness? It's mental shock that came from fear. They don't have the mentality to go to war. If they thought it was wrong to feel that way and felt bad about it, would you say that's fair?"

"That's true. But each person must be able to do at least some-thing, no?"

"That's what I'm saying, Raji. Each person has to do what they're able to do. Just like when they say, 'The Sinhala you don't know can crush the back of your head,' you can't take on things you can't do and then suffer because of it."

Raji remained silent.

She couldn't speak any more.

Kamala grasped her silence perfectly and struck her secret. "You . . . me . . . we're all affected by the war, Raji. There was a wave to flee abroad, yes. It was a way of escaping with your life. But that's not the same now. Now they go for a lifestyle, that's all. Was this our lifestyle in Jaffna? I'm not ashamed to speak the truth. For ages and ages our house was a mud hut. The women in my family never saw any gold or silver jewellery. Their bodies were never draped in silk sarees. Only handloom sarees. Where did we ever see maxis . . . or churidars . . . or mixers . . . gas cookers, pres-sure cookers, when did we see these? Our needs have multiplied in Chennai. So, we need to go abroad. I don't think we can change now. Thambiraja always said as soon as the fight stops, he's going back. Like me, I think the cold in that country doesn't agree with him. If I could stand the cold, why would I leave my man there and live here? It means, at least for that sake he still loves his own land. Maybe others will want to go back too . . . for different reasons. But not everyone will go back."

How has this woman kept her mouth shut all this time? Raji wondered in awe.

Kamala got off the ledge, as if her work was done, or as if she knew she had reached her limit. "Come, let's go downstairs. We've been up here for a while, now."

Raji followed behind her.

"I'm going to make some tea" Kamala said and walked towards the kitchen. "For me too," Raji said and went into the bathroom.

When she came out, she heard Kamala speaking to someone over the phone. "I'll tell her, akka. I was just talking to her for an hour on the balcony and giving her some advice."

" . . . "

"Okay, akka."

Kamala put down the phone and turned. "It's amma, Raji. She has confirmed her ticket. Her flight is on Wednesday. Well, do you think you'll be able to go see her before that?" she asked.

"Hm . . . "

Kamala abandoned the topic; it was up to mother and daughter now. "I made the tea, go have some."

After she had her tea, Raji called Rajanayagam on the phone.

"Hey, mahal, you haven't thought about this old man at all . . . "

"How can I not think about you at all, sir? They say each house has its front steps. That's how it is for everyone. Still, we talk occasionally when we think of each other. I'm calling you now because I'm thinking of you."

"You're calling to ask me something . . . "

"I don't call you only when I need to know something."

"Okay, okay, you're calling at this time of day, what's happening?"

She asked, "There's a story floating around that there might be peace between the Tigers and the government, what do you think of that, sir?"

There was silence at the other end of the line.

She could hear him moving, the phone crackled.

Then he gently broke the silence, "It's an illusion," he said. "It's not possible for people who are slaves to a dream to make peace. Only people who can see reality can do that."

"What's the reality, sir?"

"Reality? Misery is a reality of war. Tears are a reality of war. Hunger, deaths are a reality of war. In a world where deaths are cheap, peace will come when the disillusioned walk the earth. It will view equality and human life as parallel to each other. The only way to that is through a rebirth after the old is destroyed. The racists will not agree to it. They are trapped in a prison of their own dreams."

"What is their dream?"

"Religion . . . language . . . so much more."

"Mm," she said, absorbing his words.

"What is it, mahal, you're quiet?"

"Nothing, sir."

"Arasi called in the evening. She said she'd probably go back to the village with Thiravi after your mother leaves for Canada. But let that be . . . what are you going to do? Staying in Chennai . . . or will you run away to the camp again?"

"I can't go back to the camp whenever I like anymore, sir. Even if I could, I'm not going to do either of those things."

"Then?" He had expected something else, and his voice was pained.

Kamala, who had been switching between television channels with her remote as she half-listened to Raji's conversation, was overcome with the same feeling.

"Let me be. Do you know which animal I used to like as a child? The lizard. I didn't know that the lizard could regrow its tail back then. Now I know. The lizard can grow its tail. The lizard is not a symbol for divination, it's a symbol for trickery. I'm pretty much like a lizard."

You can shake people physically with words. The two listening to Raji's words shook then.

Raji didn't speak for much longer. She hung up, saying she would visit him in person soon.

She didn't stay in the hall either. She left Kamala adrift in her thoughts and went to her room.

17

Peliyagoda, Sri Lanka

THE KELANI FLOWED. A silence burst and spread along the river, which had never been so tired before.

It was a full moon night on the eighth of February in two thousand and one.

The night was swallowing the moon.

Gunananda was on the grassy bank. He had changed a lot in a short time. His body had grown thin as a palm rib. He looked as weak as wood turned to ash. His eyes had sunken in so deep they looked like stars reflected in the bottom of a well. Yet they burned like twin embers in a deep ditch. All that remained in his gaze were the fatigue and frailty of an ancient resentment.

There were two men with him. His band of five had scattered. It was Silva from the Deshapremi Janatha Viyaparaya who broke off first. He told them as he left that he couldn't put his faith in the bhikkhu's weakness anymore. The bhikkhu didn't stop him. The older bhikkhu had left to take on a new position of leadership without even telling them. It was six months since the ragged bhikkhu had died. It was only the young bhikkhu Rajapakse and Munesinghe from the Mawbima Surakimu Viyaparaya.

There was a dagoba across the Kelani. Even though the moon was hidden, the dagoba's rounded peak gleamed brightly.

The bhikkhu was lying down with his head resting in the crook of his arm. Once you begin to feel the effects of an incurable disease on your body, the anger against anything is doubled. The inability to vent it turns the heart into a wave-battered shore.

They hadn't met during the past few Poya days. The others came. Gunananda Thero didn't come. This might even be his last day as the leader of this band.

The sky was clear. The stars were visible.

It was the young bhikkhu Rajapakse who broke the net of silence. "Nothing seems to happen as we expect, does it, Thero?"

"How will it happen?" Munasinghe said through gritted teeth. "Action . . . action! That's the only way to accomplish anything. Thinking won't help you move even a hair, Rajapakse."

Gunanada still did not break his silence. He looked from one to the other. He was too bored to speak, even though he had thought of something to say. At one time, not so far back, even a year ago he had been able to shake that kingdom. The Sangha would get excited whenever they saw him. Now . . . ?

Without moving, or looking at anyone, the bhikkhu spoke: "What do you say didn't happen, Munesinghe? Wasn't it part of our plan for this party to be in power today? Who else could have staged that kind of theatre but us?" he asked softly.

"I'm saying that's not how it should have happened. We should have known that it was not how it would happen."

"Would the leadership of the other party have done any better than this?"

"I'm not talking about how well it does. It would have changed the type of war when it came into power. We would not have lost Elephant Pass. Even more: the lands that were a symbol of our victory and our power would not have been lost."

"Mmhm," the bhikkhu replied.

"What is it, Thero, you're so indifferent? We're losing, Thero. Our strategy is not helping even an atom," Rajapakse said.

Gunanada knew their minds. He knew that they were not going to meet like this again. He wasn't saddened by that. He had thought long and hard over the past few months and come to some clarity. He could preach it to them. If they heard it, let them hear it and go. Or, let them experience it. He didn't have to appease them.

"That is inevitable, isn't it?"

"Thero.! What are you saying . . . ?" Munesinghe was shaken. He clenched his fingers into fists.

"Why are you hissing, Munesinghe? Do you want to do something to me?" the bhikkhu asked and laughed. "I am half dead, my friends. I am not afraid of anyone now. Or anything. The time has come to accept the truths."

The bhikkhu stopped, to create an opening, as if to give them time to calm down and listen to his thoughts. Then he said: "We have abandoned justice to strengthen our position more and more, and to improve our lives."

"When, Thero?"

"In fifty-six. Or, if I am going to be more precise, in forty-eight. We are quarreling today because we rejected fairness then."

"What fairness did we reject?"

"Fairness is always the same. But we can give it all kinds of different meanings. Justice for a single person is different. And social justices and political justices are different."

"How on earth is that?" There was mockery in Munesinghe's voice.

Gunananda kept an unusual hold on his temper and smiled gently. Then he said, "What are you going to accomplish by fighting, you fools? You can't get to the truth by arguing. The law is not an absolute. It expands and expands until it becomes an absence. Then conscience has to move from that extreme. We are people who have lost our conscience in the place where law ended. We must turn away from our sins."

"Let's win the war first. Then we can talk about repentance."

"This is not a war that we can ever win."

"Why?"

"Because that land is full of warriors. They go to battle with drought and the sea every day of their lives. They don't let go of anything. That's not all. They are incredible engineers. Aren't we hearing in the news that they have discovered or innovated some missile techniques?"

"So, you're saying that this war cannot be won?"

"Yes. Not by anyone."

"Thero, we already knew that your weaknesses wouldn't let you speak in any way than this. But you forgot one thing. A war is not just carried out between the two factions involved. We are going to connect with some neutral factions. We know how to get them on board too."

They stood up eventually.

"We're leaving," Munesinghe said and began walking.

"We won't need to meet anymore. This is the last time," Rajapakse said as he followed behind Munesinghe.

Gunananda kept watching them impassively, as they faded slowly into the distance. Disease was forgotten. Age was forgotten. Loneliness, helplessness came upon him. He should have expected this. Even an ordinary person should have expected this. Despite being a monk, he had forgotten to anticipate this.

Wasn't this because he had forgotten what the Buddha said: "It is only good deeds that surround a man and guard him in his old age?" Now that age and disease had brought him low, helpless, and abandoned by everyone, the bhikkhu lay in patient thought.

Had he lived for sixty-two years? No. He had not lived even for fifty years. He had spoken about race, spoken about language, but he had not spoken of the human. Even the Maha Sangha had not asked him to speak of the human. Where did the fault lie? In him? In the Maha Sangha? In Buddhism?

He pondered.

Many large businesses put aside a percentage of their profits towards advertising throughout the year. It wasn't only to increase their business. It was to maintain a balance in their income. They acknowledge their projected profits. Those who understand the principles of business avoid excessive profits. They know that it's not the right way to grow.

Many businesses send large amounts of money to the central Sangha as if for advertising. It was inevitable that the Sangha reflected their interests.

Gunananda's mind cleared.

There was a large star in a corner of the sky.

He saw it was beginning to dawn.

But he was in no hurry.

The days when he had hurried had passed now.

He realized that he had been acting as another, for another, and it affected him profoundly.

Wasn't his entire life a failure?

Everyone had their own Bodhi tree. At some point, knowingly or unknowingly, they will sit beneath that tree. He had come to his very late. That was all.

Were there any days left to him, to feel its benefits?

As the day dawned, the bhikkhu closed his eyes.

18

Nainativu, Sri Lanka

THE GREAT BELL OF the Nainativu Nagapooshani Amman temple rang out dong . . . dong . . . creating tremors in the air. Clad in the dense mists of February, the little island opened its eyes.

The wind was harsh that day. The night dew was still heavy in the air. Above, the sky was dense with the dawn flight of crows, parrots, storks, and mynahs. Tall waves crashed against the shore. But the island was shrouded in quiet, devoid of its usual sea-bird song.

The sun rose then in the east. A clamor of bells arose from the Murugan temple in the middle of the island, the Pillaiyaar temple, and the Kali temple in the south. The peals grew into a flood throughout the island. They rose and flew as if to chase away the gloomy cold.

It was the point that marked the separation of day from night.

Just then a boat arrived from somewhere and dropped off its two passengers near the southern shore and sped away roaring to disappear in the distance.

The taller figure picked up the small figure, hoisted it on its shoulders and walked in from the sea.

The figure walked through the slimy mud, through sand, and then lowered the small figure to the ground and held its hand and began walking.

"Thiyagu maama . . . !"

"What is it, Vithu, are your legs hurting? The temple is near . . . just a little further, come."

The two of them arrived just in time for the morning poosai at the Amman temple and stood apart watching the devotees who had begun to arrive there to worship.

There was no one there that he recognized, or even anyone who recognized him. Thiyagu was shocked.

How many years he had spent on this soil. How many people he had known. For how many had he run errands, chopped firewood, chopped grass for their cows and their goats, and gathered leaves? And none of them were here today.

What had happened to the character of this island?

The Naina Amman temple, the Manipallavam Library, Manimekalai Theatre, the marutham tree on the bank of the great pond, the Naga Vihara . . . they were all the same. But the people?

Perhaps he might meet someone he recognized, or someone who recognized him in a little while, either there or somewhere else. "Who is it, Thiyagu? When did you come?" they might ask. But he couldn't get over the fact that he had felt like an alien in his land from the moment he arrived.

In this moment, he was not only a stranger, but an orphan.

Had he braved the deadly ocean to for the second time only to meet this alienation?

He had not only crossed the sea, but he had also crossed paths with death.

Yogesh had been a boatman who never flinched at anything. Yet, that day, as they left, he had said, "Something doesn't feel right, Mulla." You could put your life entirely into his hands and ask him to give it back to you on the other shore. He had such a mastery over the waters. He knew everything there was to know—the sand banks, the rocks, the leap of the waves, and the nature and direction of the winds. He could accurately predict if it was a fish or a wave that leapt in the distance. He was a child of the sea. But when the sea grew angry at the one who challenged its pride and grandeur, and roaring it sought revenge, it claimed him first. It had risen roaring against him once before too. He had escaped then.

When it rose against him that day, the Sri Lankan navy had colluded with it.

When the rounds of bullets began whirring from the navy gunboat, Mulla, Vithu, and Thiyagu had all hidden, flattened against the belly of the boat. But Yogesh had stood, steering the boat this way and that, dodging the whizzing bullets. It was a game. But it was also a technique.

The sight didn't last for long. "Ah!" an anguished cry. That was it. Yogesh leaned back. The sea raised its arms in waves, embraced, wrapped, and swallowed him. Before they realized what was happening, the boat had capsized and began to sink.

The dark helped them as they swam, hidden from the eyes of the navy, and he and Vithu reached a stretch of sand. At dawn they saw that Mulla had survived too.

It had taken many days before he and Vithu were able to catch another boat and come to the island's southern shore.

The sunbeams grew warmer, and the mist dissolved.

The whole world awoke.

Thiyagu stood there with Vithu, searching for someone he might know.

War had driven away its inhabitants, and a desolation had fallen not only on the stretch of this little island, but also throughout the whole larger island.

As they slowly walked away from the temple, Thiyagu and Vithu were just another embodiment of the island's grief.

Though it was bare and lonely, it was still his land. And Vithu's. What he felt beneath his feet was not only grains of sand, but the gravity of this soil.

The wind
Resounding everywhere
My land . . . my homeland.

Notes to Book 4 and Book 5 of *Prison of Dreams*

Anula story: A story from the Sinhala *Mahavamsa*, which depicts the queen Anula of Anuradhapura in a salacious manner.

book, head change, getting an entry, exit: the smugglers' slang for passport, photo switch, entry and exit visas.

Ceylon: old (colonial} name for Sri Lanka until 1972. Many Tamils still use the name Ceylon rather than Sri Lanka, as they see latter as a symbol of the rise in Sinhala Buddhist fundamentalism.

SJV Chelvanayakam: A Tamil lawyer, politician, and Member of Parliament who found the Ilankai Tamil Arasu Katchi (otherwise known as the Federal Party) and the Tamil United Liberation Front. He was affectionately known as Thanthai Chelva (lit. Chelva, our father).

Dutugamunu: A Sinhala king (born between 100-200 BCE) who is said to have ended the Tamil domination of Anuradhapura by killing the king Ellalan.

Eelam/Tamil Eelam: The independent state that many rebel groups hoped to form.

IPKF: International Peace Keeping Force, sent by India to Sri Lanka to help maintain a ceasefire. They eventually commited atrocities and aided the further fragmentation of the Tamil Movements.

JR Jayawardene: the former president of Sri Lanka, belonging to the United National Party; he was president during the pogroms of 1983.

JVP: Janatha Vimukthi Peramuna (People's Liberation Front), a Communist party formed in 1965 by Rohana Wijeweera. The group conducted two armed insurgencies against the Government of Sri Lanka, in 1971 and in 1987-9, with the aim of creating a socialist state.

Kantha Puranas: also known as Skanda Puranas, referring to Murugan, the son of Siva and Parvati. It is a sacred text composed by Kachiyapper, a Tamil scholar of Sanskrit, and refers to cosmology, pilgrimages, and the nature of right and wrong.

LTTE: Liberation Tigers of Tamil Eelam, a rebel group founded by Velupillai Prabhakaran in 1976, to secure the independent state of Tamil Eelam in the north and east of Sri Lanka.

Movement: The word *Movement* originally referred to the Tamil struggle in general but went on to refer to the various rebel groups in the Tamil struggle. It eventually came to refer solely to the Liberation Tigers of Tamil Eelam, after they eliminated or disbanded the other groups.

Mawbima Surakimu Viyaparaya: Sinhala fundamentalist Buddhist organization.

Nainativu: Also known as Naga Nadu (lit. snake land/island) in Tamil, and Nagadipa in Sinhala, a home of the ancient tribe of Naga (snake worshipping) people indigenous to South India and Sri Lanka. It is one of the small islands forming a cluster near the Northern Peninsula of Jaffna. It is a site of great historical and mythical significance and is referred to in the ancient Tamil Sangam epics Kundalakesi and Manimekalai as Manipallavam.

Prabhakaran: Velupillai Prabhakaran, the founder and leader of the LTTE until his death in 2009.

Special Task Force: A tactical unit of the Sri Lankan Police devised for covert operations, they are responsible for a large number of extra-judicial disappearances and killings.

Tamil Rehabilitation Organization: A group founded in 1985 by Tamils who had fled the violence in the north and east of Sri Lanka.

Theepavali: Festival of lights, celebrated by Hindus in November. It carries different meanings for Hindus of different areas and is also criticized as a celebration of the suppression of indigenous tribes.

TULF: Tamil United Liberation Front, a political party formed by SJV Chelvanayakam in 1972.

Mattavilasa Prahasana (Sanskrit): "A Farce of Drunken Sport," a one-act satire written by the Pallava king Mahendravarman in Tamil Nadu, India.

Pathmanaba: A founder of the Tamil rebel group the Eelam People's Revolutionary Liberation Front (EPRLF) who was assassinated by the LTTE in 1990.

settlement schemes: shortly after independence, the Sri Lankan government began giving land to Sinhala farmers in the more fertile regions of the country. While a small number of Tamils and Muslims also benefitted from these schemes, they predominantly worked to change the demographics of traditionally Tamil-dense areas.

Dravida Kazhakam: a caste abolitionist social movement begun by Periyar that called for an independent nation called Dravida Nadu. It gave birth to the political group Dravida Munnetra Kazhakam and All India Anna Dravida Munnetra Kazhakam.

Periyar: E V Ramasamy, called Periyar and Thanthai Periyar, was a caste abolitionist and an advocate of the self-respect movement in Tamil Nadu.

Muslim expulsion: the forced eviction from the northern province of more than 72,000 Muslims by the LTTE in 1990.

"We rose up to live": a line from V I S Jayapalan's well-known Tamil poem *Uyirthezhuntha naatkal* (Resurrection Days), written just after the riots of 1983.

PTA: Prevention of Terrorism Act, a draconian legislation passed by the Government of Sri Lanka in 1979 that became a tool for arbitrary detention and persecution of minorities, protestors, insurgents, and rebels.

Sons of the Soil: Sinhalaye Mahasammatha Bhoomiputhra Pakshaya (The Great Consensus Party of the Sons of the Soil of Sinhala) was a Sinhala Buddhist Fundamentalist nationalist party formed in 1990.

Sinhala Bala Mandalaya: a Sinhala Buddhist Party formed in 1981.

Bhoomiputhra pakshaya: formerly the Sinhalaye Mahasammatha Bhoomiputhra Pakshaya, Motherland People's Party, a Sinhala Buddhist Political party formed in 1990.

Sangha: monastic order of Buddhism, which along with the Buddha and the dharma are the basic creed of Buddhism, the threefold refuge.

Madhyamika Buddhist: the Middle Way, a school of Mahayana Buddhism, founded by the Indian monk and philosopher Nagarjuna, which recognizes truth as existing on two planes: the everyday (quotidian reality) and the ultimate (emptiness).

Parinirvana: "nirvana after death"; as one who attains nirvana in life continues into nirvana after death, they are released from the cycles of rebirth.

Q branch: a wing of the CID of Tamil Nadu police, originally formed for surveillance of the Naxal Movement.

Glossary

aacchi: grandmother or elderly woman
ahimsa: the Buddhist precept of nonviolence
aiyya, appa: father
aiyya (Sinhala): older brother
acharu: a mix of raw fruit with salt and chillie powder
akka: older sister
amma: mother
anna, annan, annai (affectionately): older brother
asoka tree: (lit. without sorrow) an evergreen tree believed to promote happiness
asura: a demon
ayubowan: a formal Sinhala greeting
bhikkhu: Buddhist monk. Also "hamaduru"
billa: a demon or bogeyman
bo tree: a tree considered sacred in Buddhism because the Buddha is believed to have attained nirvana under it
Daathu: the tenth year in the Tamil calendar cycle of sixty years. In this instance it refers to the great famine of 1876 in Tamil Nadu, India, brought about by poor distribution of food and monocultures under the British rule
double: two riders on a bicycle or motorcycle. Sometimes a motorcyclist would ride with a gun-carrying pillion rider to carry out assassinations or to intimidate people
ganga: river
heli: helicopter

iluppai: madhuca longifolia, or butter tree, whose nuts are used for the extraction of an emollient oil, and flowers are used for making an alcoholic beverage

kanchi: water in which rice has been boiled, or a thin porridge of rice or other grain

Kanthapuranam: A Saiva religious epic featuring the god Skanda redeeming the celestial beings from demons

karaiyar: a Lankan Tamil caste of Tamil people from the north and east who are associated with fishing and seafaring

Kathirgamam/Kataragama: a town famous for its shrine considered sacred by Saivites, Buddhists, and indigenous tribes of Lanka, where Kandasamy Murugan/Skanda or Kataragama is worshipped

Kavadi: a burden carried during a ceremonial dance as an act of penance, asking for blessings

Kelani/Kalyani River: a river stretching from the Siri Pada mountain range to Colombo, it has both Sinhala and Tamil names

kiluvai: commiphora caudata, or hill mango (though its fruit are not similar to the mango)

koburam: an ornately carved and often painted tower that is part of the traditional Hindu temple design

korai grass: Cyperus rotundus, also known as nut grass

kotiyas: tigers, referring to the LTTE

Lankapuri: an ancient name for Sri Lanka from the Ramayana

maama: maternal uncle, or father-in-law

maame (Sinhala): uncle

maami: paternal aunt, or mother-in-law

maaveeran: a hero; in this context someone who dies in the Movement.

machan: male cousin, also slang for close friend

machaal: female cousin or sister-in-law

malaivembu: mountain neem or margosa tree of the mahogany family

Manthikai and Nayanmarkaddu: places known for holistic treatment centres and a hospital

maravali kilangu: cassava tubers

Mareesan: the rakshasa who takes the form of a deer to lure Rama away from his wife in the Ramayana

marutham: arjun tree

mavilanga tree: crateva religiosa, also known as the sacred garlic pear or temple plant

Menik/Manikka River: a river stretching from the Namunukula mountain range down to the Indian Ocean through Yala National Park. It has both Sinhala and Tamil names.

mulmurunga: also known as Indian the Coral tree or Kalyana Murungai (wedding murungai)

Mutraveli: Mutraveli Appa shrine in Jaffna

nanthiyavettai: tabernaemontana divaricata, also known as pinwheel flower

neytal: the coastal land referred to in ancient Tamil Sangam poetry

odiyal: tuber from the roots of the palmyrah tree

oththu or **ottu**: a double reed wind instrument that produces a low droning sound, it often accompanies the higher pitched nathaswaram

paalai: manilkara hexandra tree whose wood is dense and often used for furniture

paatti: grandmother

Panchangam: Hindu calendar and almanac

pansala: Buddhist monastery

Pillaiyaar: the Tamil name for Lord Ganesh

Saamathiyam: puberty ceremony

Sanghamitta: the daughter of the emperor Ashoka, who became a bhikkuni (Buddhist nun) and went to Lanka to spread Buddhism in the mid 200s BCE.

Sannathiyan, sannathi: a sanctum where one is meant to experience the nearness of the deity

seettu: a local cooperative buying system where members pool money and take turns withdrawing amounts to make larger purchases than they could make individually

sempu: a metal vessel for holding water

siddhas: the liberated souls (Sanskrit), or masters who have attained nirvana

Somasuntharam or **Somapala**: the former is a Tamil name, the latter is a Sinhalese name, so it implies that they couldn't confirm if Soma was Sinhala or Tamil

thaali: a necklace tied around the bride's neck during the wedding ceremony

thambi: younger brother

Thamilarasi: Tamil queen, or queen of Tamil

thangachi: younger sister

thattivaan: a truck with a large, sheltered carriage for transporting passengers.

theeva: derived from the word *theeviravaatham* which means "terrorism"

thero: senior Buddhist monk

thetha: Strychnos potatorum, also known as clearing nut tree

thevadiyal: whore

Thevakumaran: a name meaning "godly prince." *Thevar* means "gods"

undiyal: an informal money remittance system set up by community members

vaakai: lebbek tree

vanakkam: "hello" (lit. "salutations")

visvasam: faith

vembu: neem or margosa tree

verty: cloth tied around the waist, worn by men

Vesak: a festival celebrating the birth, death, and enlightenment of Buddha

vihara: Buddhist temple

Author's Note

The long novel *Kanavuchirai*, translated in English as *Prison of Dreams* now comes to an end with the fifth instalment, *A New Testament*. It has been twenty-five years since the quintet was published as individual books, and ten years since it was published as a large single volume by Kalachuvadu in India. Much has changed in the politics and socio-economic conditions of many countries in this long stretch of time. The everyday life of those times is not visible in Sri Lanka today. So, as this quintet appears in English at this time, I thought it needed an author's note at first, but something else occurred to me to discourage that attempt.

It is true that a work of fiction has the power to penetrate the human heart, be it in the source language or in translation. This is why the great works of literature from around the world continue to affect us even today. Therefore, I must pay attention to the claim that the mind of the reader can absorb the work without the help of an author's note or preface.

This novel does not aim to narrate the events of the civil war that took place in Sri Lanka, the actions of the rebel groups, or the courageous deeds of the revolutionaries in ecstatic fervour. Instead, it speaks of the suffering and misery of ordinary people, their lack, their helplessness, their losses, and their vacillations. That is why it speaks of the Lankan Tamils who wandered as refugees to India, Thailand, and even to western nations like Germany, France, Italy, England, and Canada. In short, it can be described as a story of refugees. That is why its primary motivation is not to depict the war, but to seek out the reasons driving the war.

Dreams create histories; histories create wars through the people it imprisons. *Prison of Dreams* shows us this through fiction.

Regardless of the efforts of the United Nations, both civil and international wars continue even today. As one war ends in one corner of the world, another erupts in another corner. In this global situation, novels like *Prison of Dreams* continue to be necessary; and their readership will continue to grow. A novel that speaks of the impacts of war never becomes outdated.

In this moment, it's important that I share something about the form of this novel, rather than its ideas.

Set in a period of twenty-one years beginning in 1981 and ending in 2001, this novel speaks of twenty-one centuries of Sri Lankan history. The people depicted in this novel are real. Though Ponnusamy and Maheswari may not have been husband and wife, and Maheswari and Rajaletchumi may not have been mother and daughter in real life, he was someone's husband, she was someone's wife, and Rajaletchumi was the daughter of a widow in real life. Suthan is a real person; Arasi, Amba, Thiraviyam, Gunananda Thero and Sankarananda Thero are all drawn from real people who surrounded us. I have brought them together and invented relationships between them out of creative necessity.

Though I wrote the quintet in two years, these characters had existed within me for a long time, waiting to be brought into an epic tale. The novel turned into a thousand pages in print but was handwritten in more than two thousand pages. I rewrote it several times, editing, adding, and reworking it. Therefore, it demanded my extended labour as well. Perhaps because of it, the quintet has received critical acclaim and remains an artistic accomplishment. The quintet now reaches an international audience through its translation into English. For this, I thank my friend and poet Cheran, who initiated the process, Nedra Rodrigo for her skillful translation, the author M G Vassanji for his editorial work, and Mawenzi House for publishing it in such a beautiful series of books.

Devakanthan

Prison of Dreams: A Modern Classic

Every time I sat down to try and write my thoughts on Devakanthan's universe, I was derailed by the news of the bloodletting in Gaza, and the images of thousands of children's bodies shrouded in white, oozing blood. It was also a time when I had to think about the inability to see clearly or hear clearly. I had received a message from a friend in Gaza, who was partly blind and severely hearing impaired, describing how this particular moment of living with disabilities in a war zone was affecting his perceptions. Part of the reason I found it difficult to write during this time was my own experience of the onset of hearing loss in 2017, and more recently of vision loss, and I was tormented by the thoughts of what happens to the disabled during these bombings. Though far away from my friend, I am united with him in our shared experiences of war and disability. The recurring images from both the past and the present are hard to forget and make a mockery of the call "Never Again." Reading Devakanthan's magnum opus *Kanavuchirai* in this present historical moment reopens the memory of similar horrors, suffering, and trauma in an entirely different geographical context, though the geopolitical context is, unfortunately, very similar.

As a poet, I hardly write about novels, even though I have been a voracious reader of novels and short stories in Tamil and English for a very long time. I have always been envious of great novelists. It is not because I think they have a different kind of imagination from the poet's; rather, I am envious of the time and energy they are able to invest in the details and sketches of the temporal and visual dimensions necessary for a larger piece of creative work. Perhaps this envy is the reason that many fine Tamil poets have recently turned to writing novels, though not all of them have been successful. *Kanavuchirai* is a modern classic, with no parallel in contemporary Tamil fiction , dealing with history, historiography, politics, and the genocide. This quintet is part chronicle, part life story, part autofiction, and mostly a work of imagination that magnificently exceeds all traditional boundaries and notions of historical fiction. Devakanthan's careful distillation of history as well as the stylistic risks he takes have made this work a classic. *Kanavuchirai* is very powerfully and sensitively translated by Nedra Rodrigo into English in the *Prison of Dreams* quintet. It is a superb translation in the sense that she understands the nuances of geography, language, colloquialisms, family relationships, and the war. And I must say that Devakanthan is fortunate to have Nedra as a translator.

When I first read Devakanthan in the early 80s, especially *Yutthathin Muthalaam Athikaaram*, I was struck by his language, by the feelings his novel evoked, and the scent of the soil, trees, bushes, and flowers that emerged effortlessly from the story. I first met him in Tamil Nadu, India, while he was a refugee living in a refugee camp there, and I had the opportunity to receive his complete works from him. For the next few weeks, I immersed myself in reading all his writing. It is rather unfortunate that his monumental works had to wait several decades before they received the attention, praise, and celebration they rightfully deserved. I am proud to be a contemporary of such a great novelist, and to have been able to read his works, which have borne unflinching witness to the atrocity and tragedy in powerful and often poetic prose so deeply tied to the landscape. Devakanthan can be placed alongside great classic novelists in the context of war, atrocities, and genocide like Lev Tolstoy, Boris Pasternak, Ernest Hemingway, and Erich Maria Remarque. While other contemporary Tamil novelists have written about the civil war, politics, and the Tamil genocide, what distinguishes Devakanthan from them is that his political and historical imagination is markedly different from theirs. He is also unique in his sensitivity to disabilities, and peoples Kanavuchirai with characters like Thyagu, a developmentally disabled man whose mind deteriorates further due to trauma, as well as many of the young people in the novel whose experience of trauma irrevocably destroys their potential. His most recent novel, *Kalingu* further explores the lives of war amputees, drawing attention to inflicted disability as a consequence of war. Yet, his work is not only exceptional for its content, but also for its form. On the one hand, Devakanthan is deeply knowledgeable in Tamil, Tamil religions, and mythology; on the other hand, he is also well versed in Tamil poetry, both classical and contemporary. However, none of these prevent him from finding and creating new forms of language, new words and new concepts that are totally different from those of previous authors in the context of Tamil and Tamil literature. That is why his *Kanavuchirai* stands alone—magical, monumental, and historical, while transcending both history and time.

Cheran
Toronto, 2024

Translator's Note

I remember the day I showed up at the home of Nurjehan and Mr Vassanji ready to chat about how I had mapped out my future as a translator. I had translated some poetry and a few chapters of memoir and fiction and wanted to delve into prose. I had a collection of short stories I planned to start with, and Kanavuchirai, that magnum opus, would be something I'd translate five years or so down the line. I hadn't imagined that Mr Vassanji would ask me for summaries of each text and then land on Kanavuchirai—translate this one first. I returned home both elated and terrified. This was an important quintet, and though I desperately wanted to share it with the world, I was not sure I could translate it. The past five years have been a journey with the dozens of characters that people this epic, and while that journey has been at times painful and triggering, it has also been joyful and always rewarding.

Devakanthan says in his note that while the characters in his book aren't exact reproductions from real life, they exist in some fashion, and their experiences are real. It was the realism of these characters that made me want to translate *Prison of Dreams* and kept me going through the often-gruelling process of translating. I recognized people I knew in these stories; their words sounded familiar, as though from long-forgotten echoes from my own childhood. Devakanthan's attention to the details of everyday life in a Tamil village, his examination of the pulls and tugs of kinship and friendships, his treatment of disability and critique of a society's inability to treat it with care, his depiction of whole generations denied their potential, his capacity to recognize the beauty of an ideal, while being critical of where it fails to live up to its promise, all make this work a compassionate and complex rendering of a period that holds few traces in the present. The brutal war in Sri Lanka, the genocidal tactics of the majoritarian government, and its deliberate attempts to erase Tamil culture and language have meant that we do not have access to many of the touchstones of our own memories. *Prison of Dreams* becomes a reservoir of such touchstones, in telling the story of the island of Sri Lanka through a story of the micro island of Nainativu.

Nainativu is a microcosm of plurality, as it is the site of the Nagabooshani Amman temple, and the Naga Vihara. Both religious shrines reference the presence of the Naga tribe, an Indigenous tribe that existed prior to the arrival of incursions from India and underscore syncretic practices that preceded imperialism and ethnic conflict. *Prison of Dreams* is also about the relationship to the natural world, to a sense of accountability and responsibility to a homeland that is beyond a simple claim of ownership. In his poetic descriptions of the varied landscapes of Nainativu, Trincomalee, Jaffna and the south of Sri Lanka, Devakanthan suggests that war removes us from the land, rather than return the land to us. As Cheran says in his afterword, Devakanthan's language brings the scent of the soil, the trees, the bushes, and the flowers effortlessly to the reader in his work. It was important to me to try and retain aspects of this land in retaining Tamil place names, and the names of trees, sacred to us in so many ways. I imagine these names linking diasporic Tamil readers to their homelands, returning the land to them in some form, and that was a joyful exercise.

This quintet was also a pleasure to translate because of the rich inner lives of the women Devakanthan portrays here. Whether matriarch or miser, intellectual or poet, whether they dreamed of simple domestic lives or of liberatory struggle, these women were not two-dimensional characters. The tragically flawed Maheswari could still find compassion for Saraswathi's family even as her own disintegrated around her. The ambitious and stubborn Raji carves out her own morality when war and displacement make it impossible for her to live by her traditional village values. Arasi mourns the loss of her noble and beloved husband but refuses to allow her widowhood to define her life. Behind them are the women sacrificed to war and hatred, Swarna and Rakini, who remind us that the brutalities of war are often carried out on the bodies of women. Through it all, we are compelled to see the ways in which political ideologies impact the lives of everyday men and women.

Devakanthan's characters do not fall into easy narratives of ethnic purity, but are permeable to each other through relationships, spirituality, and political struggle. The saintly Sankarananda Thero cherishes a Saiva temple, the philosophical Thiravi allies with a Left-wing Sinhala journalist and creates a family with Swarna. The developmentally disabled Thiyagu begins to heal from his trauma through his care for a child but returns home to face a new trauma when he finds his village empty of familiar faces. The temple bells that open up the quintet, which are silenced for a period and begin to resound again when very few of the island's inhabitants are around to thrill to it as Raji once did, in itself tells a story of the irrevocable impact of war on heritage and culture. Devakanthan explores politics and nationalism through a range of forms, and the confusion and chaos of a young nation that turns the dream of independence and political enfranchisement into a nightmare of ethnic hatred and militant suppression finds full expression in this quintet through a range of noble and fallible characters. *Prison of Dreams* ultimately explores the limits and possibilities of human relationships even as social contracts fail around them. It takes us through a myriad of pathways of being human, and gestures to moments of transcendent generosity that will redeem us in the end.

Nedra Rodrigo
Tkaronto, 2024

Acknowledgements

Though it refers to islands on the other side of the world, this work was carried out on the traditional territories of the Haudenosaunee, the Anishnaabe, the Chippewa, the Wendat and the Mississaugas of the Credit First Nations. I am grateful to be able to do translation here and am indebted to the work of Lee Maracle and elder Laureen Blu Waters in thinking through this process. I am grateful to poet Cheran for introducing Devakanthan to me and suggesting that I translate his work, and to Devakanthan himself for trusting me with the work and for his kindness and understanding over the years when I have gone to him with questions on the historical details mentioned here.

I owe thanks to M G Vassanji who challenged me through this process, helping me become a better translator than I would otherwise, and to Nurjehan, who trusted in this work from the beginning and advised me through the arts funding process. I am delighted that Mawenzi House wanted to have these books be beautiful as well and agreed to feature watercolours by Jaffna artist Pirunthajini on the covers. The choice was an homage to the character Raji, who is a talented watercolourist, but loses track of that skill through the descriptions of her life. I owe special thanks to my multi-talented friend Dushy Gnanapragasam for agreeing to be the bilingual reader for my translations, and patiently guiding me through some of the regional nuances that I would have missed entirely otherwise. Nandri also to Mr Muttulingam and Dr Chandrakanthan of the Tamil Literary Garden for your kindnesses, and Padma Viswanathan for her thoughtful commentary when we launched the series online during the pandemic.

I am deeply indebted to my partner Paul, and our child Rafael, whose patience over the past five years has been exemplary as we juggled work, life, a pandemic, online schooling, a frozen shoulder, and translations. My friends, Brannavy, Subhanya, Geetha, Shanthiya, Jayanthi, Nimmi, Kaitlin, Shobhana, and Angela who read my translations and remind me that the work is worth doing, and my lovely global Tam Fam, I am nothing without you.

And if you picked up these books and read them, I am thankful for you too.

The Translator

NEDRA RODRIGO was born in Sri Lanka and came to Canada during the civil war. She is a translator, poet, workshop organizer, and community capacity builder, currently serving on the Board of the Tamil Community Centre project. She is the founder of the Tamil Studies Symposium at the York Centre for Asian Research at York University and founder and host of the bilingual, inclusive literary event series, the Tam Fam Lit Jam.

Nedra's poetry and essays have been published in various anthologies. Her poetry translations have been published in *Human Rights and the Arts in Global Asia; Jaggery Lit; Words and Worlds; Still We Sing: Voices on Violence Against Women*. Her translation of the memoir *In the Shadow of a Sword*, was published by SAGE YODA Press, India (2020); and her draft translation of Kuna Kaviyazhakan's novel *The Forest that Took Poison* (Nanjunda Kaadu) was shortlisted for the inaugural Global Humanities Translation Prize.